GHOST LIGHT

by Gerald de Vere

In collaboration with Mental Anarchy Press

Cover Art by Monica Kay

For more, visit spacecadetsstudios.com

ISBN: 979-8-9885955-2-6

DEDICATION

To Mark, Tom & Travis.
Thank you for providing the soundtrack to my life.

To the beautiful & cynical M.
Thank you for giving me the strength to face my ghosts.

And to my ghosts. May you find rest between these pages.

ACKNOWLEDGEMENTS

The author would like to thank the universe for the strange and challenging human experiences he's had in life, for they creep into his fiction in the oddest ways. Much gratitude is due to his colleagues and friends Chase Will of Mental Anarchy Press and Brent Winzek of Space Cadets Studios, to his cover designer Monica, and to his sensitivity readers T.T., M.K., and D.M. for their support in developing this piece.

CONTENTS

DISCLAIMER

This book seeks to address subjects of rape culture and sexual predation and therefore may contain scenes and scenarios of an upsetting nature. The author has taken great pains to handle these topics with sensitivity but understands that the subject can be triggering. Please read with caution.

For the reader seeking to do more, the publisher's professional sensitivity resources highly recommend a donation to RAINN.

EPIGRAPH

"Living systems are never in equilibrium. They are inherently unstable. They may seem stable, but they're not. Everything is moving and changing. In a sense, everything is on the edge of collapse."

– Michael Crichton

"Vero Nihil Verius."
{Nothing is truer than truth.}

– Edward de Vere, 17th Earl of Oxford

SOUND CHECK

LIGHTS UP *on the century-old* Saint Eva Theater. *Its traditional proscenium bares a proud red velvet curtain and copper frieze. The stage's dusty black floorboards are so old, you might smell the dry rot from these pages: musty teakwood that reeks of thespian wisdom far older than any living human.*

The space is bare, save for a ghost light sitting center stage. Its caged, bare bulb casts uneven cross-hatched shadows in the dark theater.

ENTER GERALD de VERE, *the bearded fool with the tortoise-shelled glasses and sandy brown hair. His cheekbones are high, his brow is hooded, and his hazel eyes are as severe as his strange name. He stares like a specter from upstage left before gliding downstage, just right of center.*

DE VERE: *Hear me, all you non-believers:*
Souls carry on; don't fear the reaper!
Gather all my ghoulish friends,
And 'fore 'ere long, we'll make amends

With all who doubt the Afterlife,
And cause our species undue strife.

For, as I studied Dionysus,
I formed this ghostly hypo-thī'sis:
College taught me many things,
Like the Death we humans bring,
And our prejudicial sting.
It taught me words were how I sing,
And antique Steenbeck editing.

Yes, life was lived more freely then,
Before I was pecked by the hen,
Still afraid to move my pen,
Still the mud in the bullpen.
But now I'm free to tell the tale
Of things you will not learn at Yale;
Yale isn't haunted like Ohio,
Where they love their Gomer Pyle.

Up northwest is where I treaded,
Where Jack Billings was beheaded.
Where my youthful heart was haunted,
Stymied still I am, and daunted.
No longer can I be mute,
This somber bard must grab his lute
To spin some truth for all to hear.
It has been well over ten years
Since I fell for the girl backstage
And stayed away, alread' engaged.

Who is to say just where I'd be,
If I had chosen dear Saidey.
I should have leapt, abandoned fears,
Instead, my duty persevered.
So, Pinky was just my good friend,
For whom I yearned until the end.

GHOST LIGHT

Those days still hurt, empty because
I'll never know where her heart was.

She stood back, made it unclear
Whether I could be her *de Vere.*
Instead, I divebombed full head-on
Into a bride of Pantheon:
Angry, depressed short blonde minstrel,
Curs'ed with a heart so dismal.

She wrapped me up and kept me trapped,
And played her mental jumping-jacks.
Never learned to misbehave,
Then dragged my heart unto its grave.
I wish I'd given up the goat:
Jumped overboard my marriage boat.
I was too young and stupid then,
to make that damn'd engagement end!

Gather ye' round, my ghosts are loose,
And tight has grown this story's noose.
The tell-tale here, most tragic, true,
Doth quickly make my verse run blue.
This journey's long, as timelines go,
And though I was with Kelly Joe,
She's not the college sweetheart here,
For Saidey's virtue drove de Vere
To pluck a quill and write this verse
Of pains brought on like star-crossed curse.

Until this night, I've blocked it out
But this November I shall shout,
Of all the things I learned at college.
For I must make it common knowledge.
I could have spared myself much strife,
If instead of my first wife,
I had chased a freer spirit…

Pink-haired, pig-tailed, phantom 'Juliet.'
Fate turnéd Shake-speare's tragic knife:
Star-crossed my heartache; grew it rife,
Birthed drama sadly solely mine.
But now, I find it most divine
To finally tell the truth in whole
About the girls who chilled my soul.

Brace yourself, it's tragi-comic,
Skeptics here will surely vomit.
May we give them little heed,
And fulfill our own souls' needs.
On with my tale of girls and ghosts;
Two things that rattle my heart most…

1. AFTER MIDNIGHT

Black Swamp, Ohio.
Friday June 1st, 2012.

'I'm bored. U up?' Her text is still hanging there in the back of my memory. I had one of those pre-smart-phone sliding Samsung deals with the hidden keyboard. Its clock confirmed: 12:41 a.m.

My heart skipped a beat.

'Yeah. Up writing,' I replied. That was true – I had been scribbling edits for a play... had been trying not to think about the girl who was now texting me.

Saidey. Her name was Saidey. And my unresolved feelings for her still chill my bones on rainy nights. Never has my own failure to act stung so hard in the long run. Be the judge of my acts but be prepared to see the tragic truth of our human condition: that, until we change a few things, any heart might easily find itself in the same painful predicament.

The text was coming from across town. I'd already been to her place once, on a lunch break back in April. She lived very near my favorite spot on-campus, the grand old Saint Eva Theatre – housed in the oldest, mustiest building on my university's grounds. Black Swamp was a dreary, rainy place with charmingly humid, cheery summers and the occasional threat of tornado. The Midwest Collegiate American Gothic Dream… and I would only be living it for a few more precious weeks. Six years of perfecting the lifestyle, and I only had one more summer in my academic Hobbiton.

After that, I was off to the wide world, like a salmon back to the sea. Off with my masters and bachelors displayed on the grill of my resume, the vehicle by which I intended to arrive at my first theater… or film… or literary job in New York City.

Gotham, that never sleeps.

How little I would sleep there.

How little I did know at that very moment, in my eagle's nest atop a townhouse full of young artists in northwest Ohio. We had our own intellectual salon, and in the preceding weeks, Saidey had leapt headlong into its atmosphere, showing far more interest than my hypercritical fiancé, a partner of nearly four years by that point.

Aye, there's the rub. You've spotted me out.

'I'm bored. U up?' Saidey's words burned my retinas, and I knew exactly what they meant. Somehow, I still doubted it, because I suffer from the melancholy and self-loathing of anxiety and depression. The symptoms were there back in 2012, though masked for all of my young life and, therefore, undiagnosed at the time. Regardless, it was bad enough to blind me whenever I was around her, or, in fact, anyone. I was in constant need of validation.

My relationship with Saidey was complicated. In the fall, we had barely noticed each other except for a few shared laughs in the scene shop, where we both worked for the theater department. Then, I invited her to a performance in early December. I was closing a particularly raunchy interpretation of *The Complete Works of William Shakespeare (abridged)* by Long, Singer, and Winfield. The invite was purely friendly – she'd helped build the sets – usually, people came to the shows to appreciate their work. I had been focused on two supporting lead roles in department theater productions, plus my graduate studies – a great majority of which I was able to supplement with my preparation for those acting roles. As it turns out, script analysis, performance and oration are indeed valuable skills for a Master of Creative Writing, whether the English department liked it or not. Spoiler: they didn't. Unbelievably, I even had to argue as much in my portfolio defense. We, the species, could talk and orate long before we were writing down our stories. I'm certain all of this was divulged to Saidey at some point. I was quite proud of that victory. At the time, Saidey seemed interested in my friend Shylock…

Yes, that was actually his name.

Shylock was a very sweet human… like if Winnie the Pooh and Al Boreland of *Home Improvement* had a kid through the miracle of gene splicing… a kid who enjoyed building theater sets. It was his blundering innocence that had prepared me for this moment. Because of Shy, I knew exactly what Saidey's text meant when it came through on June 1st. I thought back to Shylock's brush with Saidey's late-night boredom spells; in March, she'd sent a similar text to him.

We were working through lunch with Danny, our stout and jolly boss – a garden gnome of a technical director, if ever there was one. Danny and I were both acutely aware of Shylock's crush on Saidey, which had been unravelling all school year. He didn't do anything about it because we were all co-workers in the scene shop, and he didn't want to make it weird. He wasn't convinced she was into him, either.

"What did you do," we had asked in unison when he reported her text to us. I remember how jealousy twinged my heart that day. It shouldn't have. She was just a cute coworker my friend liked…

"I invited her over," he said, his cheeks blushing under his little rectangular spectacles.

"Very good," I had encouraged. It hurt to say it. For

whatever reason, I ignored the obvious reasons why.

Shylock had a difficult time with girls. He was painfully shy, which made his name tragically perfect, even though everyone loved him. "And?" I sang, swallowing the jealous lump in my throat. In that moment of jealousy, I realized I had feelings for her… feelings I immediately suppressed and redirected. In the spring semester, she and I had become friends, partly because she caught me grumbling about the other master's student we dealt with in the shop. She'd taken an interest in some film projects she caught me talking about, even expressed an interest in creating a few props, if I wanted. By March, we had become friends, but something happened to me when I'd look in her eyes… at that moment, all I knew was I wanted her to be with someone who would care for her, the way I thought Shy most definitely would… the way I wanted to.

No. Cut that out.

"And… she came over to my place," Shylock offered in response to my question after some hesitation and my profound realization.

I nodded. It stung hard, like tenterhooks sinking into my nipples. "Are you gonna' share anything else," I challenged playfully, "or do we have to coax it out of you?"

He turned beat red. Not his cheeks: his whole face. "I made soup," he said quietly.

"You what," Danny's cigarette-strained voice cracked like a surprised billy goat. It often did when he was overtly expressive.

"She was hungry," Shylock defended.

"Not for *soup,*" I shot back.

Danny guffawed.

"C'mon," Shy said, "it wasn't like that." His plea was directed at Danny.

"I'm with Jerry on this," Danny said, sipping his Mountain Dew. "Sorry, man. But that's like, flirting one-oh-one. A girl calls you – or texts – that late and says she's bored, she's after, uh..." he trailed off timidly.

"A booty call," I corrected. Danny swigged his Mountain Dew as he suppressed another laugh. "That was totally your 'in,' Shy."

Fucking idiot. I was both relieved and infuriated.

I instantly felt bad for thinking negatively about my friend. But goddammit! We'd been forming a little band of mischief-makers for our summer escapades, having been selected to stay employed by the scene shop to finish relocating the department the newly built Foxe Center facilities. Since then, I'd put extra energy into creating social opportunities for Shylock and Saidey to interact. It was admittedly an excuse to get closer to Saidey – to really get to know her. She was a cool and interesting person, she was my friend, and I wanted to be a part of her life. How didn't matter so much.

Shylock was such a painful gentleman; I could have strangled him for wasting that opportunity. He could at least tell the girl he has feelings for her and let her reaction dictate his next steps.

Easier said than done, I supposed.

Remembering that frustration in the first hour of June 2012, I appreciated the subtext of Saidey's message, re-reading it on my phone for its subtext. "It's late, I'm up, and I want to be around you."

If Shylock, the sweet but clumsy carpenter, wasn't going to taste the sweet nectar of passion, perhaps the troubled bard in graphic movie tees had a fair chance before leaving college and his youth behind.

I drafted my response. 'Yeah, same,' I confirmed, careful to leave the door open. 'Trying to write but ran out of steam.' As pretentious and presumptuous as it may seem, part of me wanted to remind her that I was an artist. From our conversations, I knew her 'type' seemed to vary, but no matter the variety, they all had a creative streak. It was also important to keep such things nonchalant.

I re-read my text: a very well-crafted response.

I hit send.

Saidey was a hard egg to crack. She was as free a spirit as the warm spring breeze, with the same wild, beautiful wonder of a glistening Manhattan sidewalk after a fresh spring rain. She was, in short, far too rad for northwest Ohio. To me, at least, she was like Punk Rock Rococo – an oil nude of a Swedish beauty from 1729 come to life, adorned with bi-lateral French Braids, a military cap, and a profound reflective depth that made her seem somewhat disconnected. She was counterculture, she was a sculptor, and she possessed eyes that had been carved from the boldest aquamarine crystals. When we interacted, I got lost swimming in them. They were framed by porcelain cheeks with perfect dimples that danced to the beat of my humor.

Her hair was pink. It wasn't always pink… as a matter of fact, it had been dark burgundy red for most of the year, which also flattered her. When she showed up to work with the pink hair, I had been shocked, but only because it was strikingly bold and vibrantly attractive. Between that, the black graphic tee and her white and turquoise checked shorts, she walked into the scene shop that morning looking like the cover art for the self-titled Blink-182 album. Having spent my adolescence as a suburban punk rock reject, artsy counterculture girls were always enticing – no matter how sharp their edges.

That morning, Danny started calling her 'Pinky' to tease her for the choice, but she liked it. "It makes me think of *Pinky and the Brain.*"

"Do you have an opening for 'Brain,' because I'll audition for the part," I had said with a grin.

"Wouldn't that be Danny," she asked.

"No – he's the scientist who's got you locked up."

"Oh, yeah. Good point."

"I'd like the part. Here: ask me what we're going to do

today," I told her.

"What are we going to do today?" She hadn't caught on yet, so she sounded confused by her own question.

I mustered my best Maurice LaMarche doing Orson Welles for the response. "The same thing we do every day, Pinky: Try to take over the shop!"

She laughed, and we broke into a rendition of their theme song. "They're Pinky – they're Pinky and the Brain-Brain-Brain-Brain." For the rest of our time together that summer, she was Pinky and I was Brain. The gag didn't persist every day, but it withstood our inside jokes for quite a while. I remember it any time I encounter those damned cartoon lab rats.

☙ ❧

I paced around my room – the master of a three-bedroom, two-bath townhouse with a full basement hangout and lofted lounge. My room was one of the coolest spots in the house: I had an antique green steamer trunk, dark wood writing desk, and shelves of books and films, all of which made it an intellectual sanctuary, and eclectic maritime décor and plant life added the charm of a Victorian study.

I am a very old soul with antiquated taste.

Indeed, all the common spaces had been orchestrated and decorated by me. It was one of the coziest places to collaborate or rehearse with peers. In just one year, it hosted three play readings of mine, a screenplay reading for Ash, three graduate student lighting technique photo shoots, a two-month-long Dungeons and Dragons campaign, and countless movie nights. Yet Kelly Joe, my affianced, never wanted to be there. She judged my friends most harshly, just as she judged every corner of the performing arts program at Black Swamp. It was paradoxical, given her complete lack of natural talent. She always wanted notes, and I always thought she seemed like she was forcing it. Her performing was stilted; it always felt to me like a fabrication. Kelly had, in point of fact, a knack for music and a lust for acting. Like so many of her appetites, what a sorry, misplaced lust it was.

I checked my phone. No response from Saidey just yet. It had only been two minutes, though. My mind tended to race that fast. I re-read that cryptic combination of letters she'd sewn together.

'I'm bored. U up?' As I read it yet again, I couldn't help but smile. I'd never had a text like that from a girl. The fact that it was *her* felt amazing. Were we about to… uh…

Guilt pooled in my gut. There was my conscience creeping in. The phone buzzed in my hand, and I jumped with a start, swinging the cell down at my side. I made myself wait a second before picking it up.

'Right? I feel antsy,' she replied. That felt overt – tickled my guilt strings even more. The ground felt like it was slipping away from me. She'd lit a beacon for the bard.

Feverish guilt washed over me as I considered my wild westerner. How often had Kelly Joe pushed me to my limits? How often had she overlooked the advances of other young men as purely innocent or friendly? And how oft had they turned predatory, as I warned they would? One hundred percent of the time. The answer was, indeed and indefatigably, one hundred percent of the time. That cycle had already started again with the guitarist at her summer gig. Reminded of that element to our argument, I steeled my resolve.

'Well, we can't have that,' I replied after a minute. It felt flirty and suggestive, and it felt good.

Swells of guilt washed over me again like a hot, salty wave of ocean water knocking up my nostrils. This was a chance to be alone together, to selfishly confirm what I'd been afraid to admit all spring; there was a storm of emotional entanglement roiling between the two of us and I was scared shitless of 'the rest of my life' with that other stubborn someone. For some reason, though, I had to confirm that the thunderclaps between Saidey and me were getting closer together.

'Have any ideas,' she replied right away. Yes, and I had a hunch she had an idea this close to one A.M., too. But she wasn't inviting me over. That was okay; there were plenty of dark corners in Black Swamp where we could be alone in the witching hour.

I thought fast. This girl liked whimsy – she was a 3D & sculpting artist with a history of glassblowing… in *high school*. I found that so impressive that she had to correct me when I'd talk like she still studied glass blowing. It had been downgraded to something she tinkered with as a hobby.

'When was the last time you took a late-night creep around campus to see what buildings were open,' was my follow-up question. It was something I loved to do, and I had a master key to U-Hall[1], that grand old musty building where the newly abandoned theaters were.

'You think anything is actually unlocked?'

'I can think of several buildings right now,' I teased. 'Plus, I have a master key to the old theaters.'

'Okay, that's pretty dope. I'm in.' My heart skipped two beats. Both theaters allegedly had a ghost; any self-respecting theater building has at least one. Hopefully, those two left us alone.

Had Saidey ever been on a ghost hunt? Was she into that? I'd share the suggestion in person. What better way to stir the chemistry than to confront mortality and potentially spark a jump-scare? I bet none of her proto-hipster fine art suitors had made such an impression. I always felt that the majority of those boys thought too highly of their own profundity.

Life is experienced through storytelling, and I always wanted to be a story worth retelling. It was also, I suspect, a way to show her my true weirdness… to offer her the

---

[1] The student shorthand for 'University Hall,' the oldest building on Black Swamp's campus.

reflective, morbid side of me and see whether or not she turned and ran.

Furiously, I typed my response. 'You wanna' meet…' my thumbs fumbled, but before they could, she sent another message.

'Can you pick me up?' My heart leapt through the ceiling. She only lived three blocks from our destination. That was another positive detail of our flirtatious gymnastics. The light of hope in my heart flickered like the lonely ghost light I was about to reveal to her in the grand old Saint Eva Theater.

'Yeah, of course,' I typed with the dumbest grin across my cheeks. 'I think I remember the spot, but what's your address again?'

While I waited, I brushed my teeth and changed into something that would match her edgy artist vibe. For some reason, I chose my black zip-up Ninja Turtle hoodie. It was colorful, but just punk enough. I fussed my hair and slipped outside without needing to explain myself to any of my roommates.

Off I raced, to Saidey's crystal eyes. I would be in their ethereal presence in a matter of minutes. They signaled in the infant morning shadows of my imagination like the guiding beacon from a tired old lighthouse. A beacon in the darkness, indeed, just like the ghost light I was speeding off to bathe her rosy cheek bones in. Before I could second-guess myself, I was cruising off in my dirty copper SUV, cranking Blink-182's *Dude Ranch* album as my naïve heart charged headlong into its very own Shake-Spearean Tragedy.

2. PATHETIC

Over a decade later, there's a younger part of me that refuses to surrender the potential energy that singed the air around my vehicle that night. I still can't get that part of my young self to let go; He's still roving those swamps in that copper SUV, wondering if he should make a move… questioning what would happen when he did.

Unwittingly, I sped towards the cleaving of my heart's deepest wound as Mark Hoppus and Tom DeLonge sang my truth: "I know I'm pathetic, I knew when she said it. A loser, a cocksucker she called me when I drove her home…"

My fiancé had indeed, on occasion, told me I was pathetic. At that point, though, I don't think she'd called me a cocksucker… yet. But she would, in due time. What a terribly homophobic phrase. I use it only to illustrate the truth of our troubled culture, and the true nature of my now-ex-wife.

She told me the people I hung out with were pathetic when she was angry or when I was depressed. She also hated my music. Any group with pop appeal and men singing was a 'boy band' to her folk-fucker palette.

I rolled down my windows and sang along.

"Don't pull me down, this is where I belong," I kept singing, "I think I'm different, but I'm the same and I'm wrong."

These were my last fleeting months in the bosom of mass-market academia – the mark of my generation's education – and Kelly Joe wasn't around to rain on my parade. All the better to enjoy it on my terms, with the people who mattered *to me.*

The whole town of Black Swamp was a simple grid, with a north-to-south Main Street, and an east-to-west Brüster Street to split the town into quadrants. I lived in the northwest quadrant, and I was headed to Saidey, who lived just a few blocks south of East Brüster, in the southeast quadrant. I could've taken North Main and crept slowly to her twenty-five miles per hour, but instead I cut due east from Wayne Manor[2], onto nearby Poe Road, where there was no urban development and a higher speed limit. Next, I turned right, tracing the western limits of our campus along Thurstin Street. Black Swamp had long since become my home. I'd spent summer breaks, winter breaks, and even a spring break hunkered in that town. It was the first town I rented property in and the first town I had a paid writing gig in. Every corner, every shadow made me crave its knowledge. The secret truths of the universe seemed just out of reach in the shadows of those academic halls, but navigating its roads was a skill I'd long since honed by car and on foot.

Turning left onto East Brüster took me round the corner of Pensive Hall and jarred me into the past. I had lived in those dorm suites for two years of undergrad, and I'd met Kelly Joe while residing there. That had already been four years ago… or it would be four years in the fall… in just a few short months. We met in the exact same theater I was about to share with

---

[2] My townhouse lair's playful nickname. The basement was lovingly dubbed "The Bat Cave" for its ultimate 'nerd cave' energy. I played D&D for the first time in that basement: a most excellent pad, Wayne Manor.

someone else.

ɞ ɞ

Kelly Joe and I first encountered each other in the Saint Eva Theatre in the fall of 2008. It had been her first semester, and she was already a shoo-in for the department production I was assistant directing. That was because she played mandolin, and the director needed musicians. We were mounting William Shake-Speare's *A Winter's Tale* for the Holiday season, and we were framing it as though a traveling Victorian theater troupe were telling it just before Christmas, 1843. I had joked with Geoff, the director – who was my mentor and surrogate parent at that point – that perhaps our troupe was trying to capitalize on the Dickens publication's recent popularity.

"This is why you're my A-D," he exclaimed. "That's exactly my creative concept!"

I grinned.

Those first few months with Kelly Joe once felt special. Painful for so many reasons, including the grief of losing a childhood friend and a grandfather over the holidays, and how I had to fight to keep Kelly Joe around. I hadn't been good enough for her back then. Was I good enough now? We were always fighting, and she was always upset with me for something. Usually something abstract that reflected her own internal issues, but hindsight is twenty-twenty, and at that time, I thought there was something wrong with me.

The theater and its ghosts had been accepting of her presence and her talents back when she was new. Back then, she still believed in ghosts. But, as with anything in life, she had changed. She didn't believe in anything anymore… anything except herself, that is. The world was what it was; there was nothing more – no spiritual element to existence – a true dive off the deep end of her Bible-Bra upbringing[3]. If the ghosts in the Eva had sensed that in the past year or so, perhaps they'd give me space with Saidey.

People always seem nicer – better – when you first meet them. Familiarity doth breed contempt. My fiancé and I were, frankly, no fun together. We had struggled for almost two years. In truth, we got closer because Kelly Joe's friends seemed to be decreasing in quantity. Some of my friends had flown the coup, too. Familiarity, indeed.

The track switched, the CD player set to shuffle, and I let songs from my truculent adolescence carry me forth with reckless abandon. "It's all right to tell me what you think about me," I sang along, "I won't try to argue, or hold it against you."

I disconnected from thoughts of Kelly Joe as I drove to Saidey's. And so, I sang:

"I know that you're leaving.
You must have your reasons.
The season is calling;
Your pictures are falling… down."

Not only did I like my chosen route for the view and the quiet, but it had less traffic lights. I was outside Saidey's place in seven minutes tops, the lyrics to blink's *Dammit* sparking ruminations about how a breakup with Kelly Joe might playout. She'd stirred the shit earlier that night and gone drinking with her new musician friends. I had no doubt they'd only last the summer, for that was another lamentation of Kelly Joe's… friends didn't seem to hang around long. Whatever.

She was stressed about learning music for a Cedar Point show she was strumming in… she still couldn't sight-read music to play her mandolin. She was a great musical improvisor, and getting better, and she had no problem sight-

---

[3] For which, none should fault her.

reading music for vocal performance… except for all the notes she couldn't hit. Her voice often sounded locked and strained, but I suspect that was all the clenching she insisted she didn't do.

That was Kelly Joe, though. She was as bull-headed as the sows her father reared. For some reason, I found that stubborn streak endearing. Challenging. I'd never felt like I had to work to win someone over. Kelly Joe seemed to demand it.

How long would I chase?

How much would I tolerate?

How much could she hurt me before I'd run away?

Enough of that, and enough of Kelly Joe. Rounding the bend onto Saidey's street, I shook my troubles from my head.

As I pulled up, the front door to Saidey's little white rental house opened and she ran out to my passenger door, smiling as her pink braids bobbed over her shoulders.

She didn't have her hat on. That was the first time I'd seen her socially without her black military cap: the same hat she wore religiously to work every day of the week. The one she wore a month prior, when I'd hosted a B-movie screening for the shop crew…

☙ ❧

Friday April 27th, 2012.

It had been a night of simple collegiate ideals… a night to remember. It was exactly the kind of experience I was seeking more and more as my days of tenure dwindled with the rising summer heat. It was my first chance to unleash the latest household B-movie discovery on a group of unsuspecting friends, much like my childhood hero, Dr. Clayton Forrester. The vintage VHS mess I experimented on them with? *Yor: The Hunter from the Future.*

Our roommate Bushel had discovered it via some dude's B-movie vlog and ordered a DVD copy. We laughed so hard we cried. Before he moved out at the beginning of April to go live with his fiancé down in the Gulf, he made me a copy as a parting gift. When I told the crew at the shop about it – Saidey, Danny, and Shylock – they were all intrigued. We planned the screening for April 27th: the Friday before finals week.

I couldn't wait to host everyone that night, and festivities kicked off right after work. Since we were ordering pizza for dinner, everyone except Danny just followed me home. Danny had a family, and he had to go check in with them and be a dad first. He had my address and joined us shortly after.

The rest of our crew, though, walked across campus, over to the lot where I parked for a nice long walk in my mornings. Along the way, we joined up with my buddy Big Jay.

Big Jay was a huge Trekkie, a classy graphic designer, and had impeccable taste in films that matched my own. His prominent brow and strong profile gave him that rugged, American Classic look – like a young, suave John Goodman. He was a force, Big Jay. Six-foot-three, three-hundred pounds and sharp as a whip, he had been an Offensive Tackle all through high school football on a competitive Ohio team. In college, he gravitated towards the arts, which had planted us squarely in the same social circles.

The group of us there on April 27th already knew each other from lunches shared, and everyone exchanged greetings as they piled into my vehicle. As soon as we got in, Saidey started cackling in the back seat.

"What," I asked.

"Vanilla cupcake," she asked back, pointing at my air freshener.

I felt my cheeks ignite with pigment.

Big Jay shifted only enough to regard her from his usual spot in the front passenger seat. If you were hanging with Big Jay and me, you rode in the back seat. That was just how it was. We were locked in as designated co-pilots.

"What's wrong with that," Big Jay asked, unamused as he

nodded to the air freshener hanging from my rearview. "Smells good in here." Big Jay always had my back, even when he didn't realize it. We were gentlemen and scholars, with fine taste, you see. Sure, we were also working-class goons in our early twenties, but we appreciated keeping things classy.

Saidey, somewhat subdued, but still in good fun, replied, "I just wasn't expecting it," she said. "It's cute that you have a vanilla cupcake side."

I watched the color drain from Shy's face.

Oops.

Then, I started my engine, and the speakers kicked on, blasting Mozart's *Symphony No. 25 in G Minor, K. 183: I. Allegro con brio*. I hadn't turned off my music and prepped for driving everyone… for having Saidey in my car for the first time.

Shit!

Saidey tilted her head to the side inquisitively, finding my eyes in the rearview mirror.

"Vanilla cupcake *and* classical? I'm learning so much about you, Jerry."

"Mozart's great to start your day to," Big Jay attested.

"Definitely easy on the mind," I agreed. "I like classical, but I'm not *entrenched in it*, you know? I can barely name anything. I just recognize a few composers by style. So, I know Mozart's my favorite, but I can't name any of his stuff," I said with a shrug. "However, tonight we need something a little more upbeat." I swapped the *Amadeus* soundtrack for my homecooked blink-182 disc. Rock Show played us out as I drove us north to pick out alcohol.

There was beer and pizza aplenty, and I don't know that I've ever enjoyed a B-movie screening quite as much as that glorious night. The sun was casting its clementine glow through the sliding glass door out to our patio, and the air was fresh, so I had the windows open. We all got high on life and fermented hops and guffawed at an ill-fated cinematic disasterpiece of prehistoric proportions.

I spent a lot of time on the floor or on my feet, eager to serve more drinks and pizza. The sun set on my last real semester in Black Swamp as it dipped beneath the horizon outside my cozy artists' den, and all was right with the world. The embers of a promising future were burning bright that fateful night and, in between movies, I got the hint that a budding summer heartache was also rolling in – my very own Tropical Storm Saidey.

After *Yor* was done, we were all still game for more cinema trash, so I offered the Mystery Science Theater classic *Space Mutiny* starring Reb Brown, who we had just watched as Yor. Ever the professor, I explained how he was the original Captain America, and how he really didn't do anything of note in Hollywood after that. Instead, he did weird international sci-fi parts like Yor, the muscle-blond super caveman and Strider, the muscle-blond super space soldier.

We took a break between films for refills: the beer was gone, and Danny was hoping to buy a new pack of cigarettes, so I led the way two rural blocks north to the nearby gas station. Saidey fell into step next to me, and Edwyn, my short, pony-tailed roommate & confidant since freshman year, trailed us until he, too, caught up. Shy, however, hung back, chatting with Danny about his summer gig at the Huron Playhouse, out near Port Clinton.

"Just us in the shop this summer, Pinky," I teased Saidey. I knew from our conversations over lunch that she had also extended her shop work into the summer.

"Thank God I have you," she said, tugging my arm. "Otherwise, after Shy leaves, I'd be stuck with Vance and Thad all summer."

"Please," I teased, "he prefers *Thaddeus*." Thaddeus Flick was a particularly pedantic dunce, a lanky classmate from the graduate program who had weaseled his way into shop work for the summer even after he hadn't initially been selected. It was because he was a fuss and because his mouth worked double-time on his complaints, which slowed his soft, spindly hands to a snail's pace with the woodwork.

I suspect the fact that he smelled like a dirty pillowcase also turned people off, whether or not they realized it. His wife was allergic to something in most soaps and detergents. I can't recall what natural soap concoction they used to clean their fabrics, but it didn't work. Summer heat and sweat would only worsen that. A tuft of curly brown hair and a sullen brow gave him the severity of a Dr. Suess antagonist, and his body posture followed suit. He viewed the world through a harsh Midwestern Baptist lens and was often excruciatingly judgmental. It didn't groove with anyone in the liberal arts: his peers, the undergrads, or his professors. He was going to be 'extra.' We were moving the rest of the theater supplies in storage, and Danny needed a solid team. The man was in charge of relocating nearly a century's worth of department property and equipment from University Hall. They were doing that because the university intended to tear down the old theaters... *my* theaters.

"But yes," I said to Saidey, "you're stuck with me all summer." It was true. I had summer classes until mid-July, then a portfolio review, then graduation wasn't until the first week of August. Black Swamp got pretty desolate in the heated months, and though I had enjoyed the peace in years past, I found myself extraordinarily restless that year; I was unwilling to sit inside alone for my last glorious summer in my adopted home.

I settled into Saidey's touch just in time to lose it. But she had squeezed my left biceps. I'd been lifting and moving shit in the shop all year, and I was confident she had noticed.

Guilt rushed through my veins, but I quickly recovered. My fiancé was off pickling her liver in Cedar Point, forcing herself to learn how to read sheet music for her instrument, and to generally ignore me. I was backseat to a gig, a trend that would only worsen with time. But for now, I was free... free to grow close to the girl with glass-blue eyes and cotton candy hair…

Some time back in late March, I'd coerced Saidey and Shy to join me for lunches at the new on-campus Dunkin. We were always brainstorming some short film or working on the sci-fi saga he had started giving me notes on. That trickled over into lunches, and Saidey expressed an interest in a short we were cooking up. After a few lunches, she was onboard to make several prop weapons for it, namely some futuristic firearms. That was how she ended up in my orbit: how things were set in motion. We were collaborating creatively, a bliss I did not know with Kelly Joe. When she tried working with me, we just got frustrated, snippy, and eventually gave up after an hour. There was always a tension there – a competition – but with Saidey, it was just unbridled imaginations riffing on each other's suggestions. I hadn't known what that was like, and perhaps it was one of the reasons I fell for her. That, and her eyes, of course…

We arrived at the gas station convenience store. Feeling the buzz that night, I chose to celebrate with a strawberry-flavored cigarillo. I checked out, and Saidey complimented my choice.

"Oh, you like?"

"I mean, in general I prefer the green stuff," she hinted. "But yeah – fits tonight's mood," she said with a smile.

"Hey, same, but I wasn't gonna' pull out the Jamaican Pine with Danny here."

Saidey laughed. "Oh my god, what did you call it?"

"You heard me," I said playfully.

"I sure did, *grandpa*!"

"Wordsmith," I flirted back, holding out a steady and pretentious hand to gesture at myself. "There are so many good nicknames for marijuana. Why be satisfied with *weed*?"

Saidey just kept laughing, shaking her head at me all the while. I waited until we were crossing back through the grassy field to light the cigarillo and offer her a taste.

"Yeah," she asked, her eyes lighting up.

"Of course," I said. "I shouldn't finish one of these by myself anyway." We walked together in silence, sharing the cigarillo. Edwyn treaded shortly behind us, professing that he enjoyed the smell. "Shy's expressed an interest in trying the Devil's Lettuce."

Saidey snickered. "Devil's Lettuce is a good one," she said to herself.

"I told him I could arrange something for him if he wanted to try it – that seemed to be what he was asking."

"Can I help? I've got to see that."

"Hell, yeah. Is that even a question? We can give him a proper sendoff." Shy was leaving for the Huron Playhouse gig in a few short weeks – his last day in the shop was the Friday that kicked off Memorial Day weekend.

This was, of course, an excuse. I desperately wanted to be alone with Saidey – to truly become friends – friends who sought each other's company. Perhaps I also hoped for some emotional trip that would send me flying out of my present situation and into Saidey's orbit.

My own experiences with reefer madness only dated back to the previous summer. I had had a moving experience with ganga and the constellations thanks to two of my grad school colleagues. They were the cool kids in the theatre master's program, both in their thirties and versed in their shit. We'd smoked in the middle of a corn field, sprawled out on the hood of a convertible Volkswagen Bug, and I named as many constellations as I could (which was maybe five).

In more recent months, I was intrigued to discover that our new roommate for spring and summer, Eric Batsford, used it to unwind. He was quite bright, and I felt a kinship with him like one might for a protégé. He reminded me of myself as a freshman, and he came in with the same strong and favorable impression. What I didn't know until he moved in was that he was the designated stoner of the freshman musical theater class, too. He divulged so I'd know it was in the apartment. I respected him immensely for that, and I exercised no qualms about huffing the fumes of philosophy with him from April to August. It was the rebellion I'd never embraced as a teenager.

"He's never had it, huh?" Saidey nodded in Shy's direction. Then she considered my proposal. "I'm excited," she said, flashing her smile. "We'll make it great. Having the right snacks is important."

"I was planning to host," I blurted out. "We have Kroger right across the street, so we could shop for snacks beforehand and surprise him." Our resolve was set, and just a few weeks later, on Thursday, May 17th, Saidey and I organized Shy's blind date with Mary Jane.

Saidey came over as soon as we got let out of shop for the day. She seemed eager, and we went to the store before Shylock showed up. It was just the two of us, and we picked out a bunch of junk, including cheese puffs, sour candies, and those little tubs of store-bought cotton candy. Saidey loved the cotton candy. I had never been with a girl who liked that stuff, but I secretly loved it; there was something punk rock about suburban store-bought cotton candy in the middle of summer – it reeked of MTV video fodder from my youth. I remember telling her the pink cotton candy resembled her hair. She took it as the compliment it was intended to be.

She paid very little attention to Shy that night – Edwyn also observed her sitting near me and generally keeping me in proximity. Hell, she even crashed on the futon that night, and rode to work with me the next morning. That was the first time I got to see her apartment; we stopped at her place so she could change clothes and wash her face. I waited in a living room scattered with different sculpting projects and unfinished academia. Tools, paints, clay, and home improvement supplies guarded every surface and corner of the common room. I fumbled with my posture, trying to look effortlessly at ease.

What a joke. But the whole morning felt like the threshold of some new, undiscovered part of myself. It felt so right – like the team effort I craved with an intimate partner. The sun was shining, glowing golden pink in the early morning, and I still recall her exclaiming with delight when I parked my car in the staff lot right by the Foxe Center's loading docks. Student parking was all scattered on the fringes of campus. Only faculty, staff and special visitors got the interior spots. Graduate students working for the university were considered staff.

We even walked in to work together, rife with new inside jokes, like referring to smoking pot as 'Playing Halo' because of a goofy gamer door sign we had for the basement. It aggressively read, 'Do Not Enter: I'M GAMING!' She thought it was hysterical.

It felt like we *had* been intimate, the way her energy shifted. She didn't care that we showed up together, didn't care that she glowed like someone who'd finally broken the sexual tension with another. If only that were true – we hadn't done a thing. Could our boneheaded bonding have caused such a stir in her? I may have been imagining things, but she seemed to walk a little taller that morning.

I was praying Shy wouldn't notice.

Unsurprisingly, he didn't. Thank the Universe.

But I cannot say the same of Danny. It was a wiggle of the moustache and a raised eyebrow as he finished packing his cigarette carton that gave me pause. His observation was not accusatory, so I pretended not to notice.

That excursion had been the first clear sign that Saidey's tides had shifted shores…

3. THIS IS HOME

There had been dozens of clear signs over the past month, and yet, as Saidey waved cheerfully to me in the glow of my headlights on the night of June 1st, those signs scattered in my mind, ducking into the shadows of insecurity.

When the brim of her cap wasn't casting its mysterious shadows, her eyes shined like the Milky Way, even under Black Swamp's jaundice-orange streetlamps. I smiled as she hopped in, but the first thing she said was, "Everything okay?"

My resting bitch face strikes again, I thought. Why was de Vere so severe? I just wanted to let go. To be fun and spontaneous and someone she'd remember… no matter what was about to happen.

"Yeah," I said with a smile. "Just up in my head about another argument."

"You wanna' talk about it?"

"It's nothing new. Another complaint lodged regarding my inadequacies." I was unwittingly opening the door emotionally. We'd done this a few times.

"I hate girls who do that," she said. "I'm sorry."

"It's okay," I said, waving it away. "We're here about

distractions," I said in my finest obnoxious British caricature accent. "There's boredom to be cured! I much prefer this to sitting up and trying to write, and it certainly beats hen-pecking, don't you think?" I gave my caricature a guttural snort-laugh and grinned my stupid crooked grin, the one with the mischievously skewed left dimple that made me look like a scraggly jackal. A chorus of her giggles harmonized with my music.

Deftly, I twirled round the steerage of my muddy bronze chariot and wove a quick path over to the U-Hall parking lot. "What's your take on ghosts," I threatened as I threw the vehicle into park. I leaned over, waggling my eyebrows in mock-fright.

She shrugged. "I don't believe in that stuff."

Challenge accepted, I thought. If anything was going to change her mind, it was the Saint Eva Theater after midnight. I'd witnessed some seriously scary shit in those old buildings, particularly in the last year or so.

"Don't say that inside. You'll piss off Alice," I warned.

"It's a girl?"

"Yeah. Former actress."

"Of course it is," she said, rolling her eyes. "Here, tell me the story first," she said, pulling her legs up to her chest on the seat and producing her little smoking pipe and a stash. She packed it and lit it, and as the embers burned between us, I ignored the lump in my throat... the part of me that remembered how Kelly Joe and I once sat in a different car in that very parking lot on our own fate-less first date.

"As the story goes," I led in, "there are *two* ghosts in these buildings... the very ones you've been working in all year."

Saidey laughed and shook her head. She was unfazed.

"The first was a girl named Alice who went through the theater program here back in the 1950s – back when there was only one theater. She was a sophomore in her first lead role – I can't remember which show – and rehearsals tend to run late because they have to happen after classes are done for the day. So, Alice was in the program with a senior named Brian, whose ghost is referred to as 'The Man in Tan' because he's always seen wearing all khaki."

"What?" Saidey laughed with incredulity. "Was he a safari guide or something?"

I laughed. "I have no idea. Maybe they were doing *South Pacific*? Brian's thing was that he would walk the girls home after rehearsals because it was late, and this side of town didn't have a lot of streetlights at the time. That was all closer to Main Street. So, the Man in Tan –

"Brian."

"Brian, yeah. He'd always wait after rehearsals and walk in a group with all the young ladies who didn't have a date to see them safely home."

"Cute," Saidey said with a snort. She took another hit.

"So, as the story goes, there was a night when the group left without Alice, not realizing she was still inside the theater. This was during final dress rehearsals, so just a day or two before the show was supposed to open. Everyone gets a little edgy and stressed, right?"

"Yeah, I noticed. Even Danny relaxed after the shows were over this year."

I shrugged. "It's part of the cycle with theater," I said honestly. Saidey offered the pipe to me. I hit it and handed it back to her.

"Alice gets left behind," Saidey prompted.

"Right. And Brian leaves with the group. Alice comes outside, can't find the group, waits around a bit, then decides to just head home herself."

"I can see where this is going."

"Yeah, it's not a happy ending. According to the story – and it *is* just a story – she was taken advantage of. Some creep followed her into her home and," I cleared my throat, "got too rough, and strangled her while he was, well…"

"Fuck," Saidey gasped.

I just nodded. "But in theater, the show must go on. And it did. Alice's understudy opened the show – at the time, Alice was just M.I.A. So, the show goes on, and weird shit happens with the electrics, and one of the flies breaks during Thursday's opening performance, then a light crashes to the floor on Friday night and nearly clobbers a kid. And no one can figure out why the show seems cursed. Then, that Saturday morning, Alice's parents are in town to see her show. They go to her place first, right? They find her body during the Saturday matinee. The cast finds out after their performance." I paused. It wasn't meant to be for dramatic effect, just the right moment for a somber beat.

"What? What happened?"

"Well, all the cops said at the time was that she had an 'accident.' The department decided to finish the show's final performance, that Saturday night, in Alice's memory."

"That's a bit twisted."

"Apparently the cast wanted to keep going," I shrugged. "There's a lot of work and resources put into a live show."

Saidey nodded thoughtfully. "What about Brian?"

"Brian found out during the dinner break between shows. He went on one last time that Saturday night. But he felt responsible for what happened to Alice. There's also a version of the story that suggests they might have had a budding romance. Either way, he feels personally responsible for her death, keeps it to himself all that night, and then, after the final performance, he hides in the theater and, so as not to curse future performances, hangs himself in the construction zone below the Eva, where the smaller venue was still being built.

"Everyone always sees Alice in the Saint Eva, the upstairs theater, and they see Brian – the Man in Tan – fucking around in the smaller theater, the Joe C. Greene… Stage managers even have a ritual where they have to wait here all alone the weekend before an opening and invite the ghosts to our shows."

"Seriously?"

"Yeah. I thought it was bull, too, but I've confirmed with just about every student stage manager we have. If they don't, our dear phantoms take it personally and wreak havoc. There are decades of stories about stage managers who didn't take it seriously and had to apologize to the ghosts to save their shows. As soon as the ghosts are invited, it stops the technical problems."

"Okay," she said, tucking the pipe in her hoodie. "C'mon, let's see if you can prove any of this." She turned and kicked her door open, and we were off on our adventure.

We slinked through the parking lot shadows up to the southeast stairwell – considered the 'back' entrance. After six years of late-night rehearsals in grand old U-Hall, I knew that particular stairwell stayed unlocked at all times because there were three old buildings separating the grand University Lawn from the theater parking lot. On colder nights, a brief layover in the bowels of that boiler-heated U-Hall lobby was the only thing that kept the bones from freezing through.

The whole of the building was shaped like a lopsided '+' with a shortened left (or western) vertex when viewed from above. That was the front of the building. The theaters comprised the right (or eastern) vertex, parallel with Brüster Street. The hallways and classrooms for the first three floors existed along the vertical vertex of the '+,' and the theater entrances met the first, second, and third floors where the vertices of the '+' met.

Right through the stairwell we passed, then popped out into the hallway on the bottom floor. Just beyond us, if we had continued to the front of the building, was a grand marble staircase trimmed with black iron handrails that climbed up to the second level, where the grand Saint Eva Theater's entrance was front and center, alongside the department box office. I loved that stairwell – fell in love with the theaters right there in that lobby when I was in high school – but tonight it made me shudder.

Kelly Joe and I had spent a good portion of our first night out together sitting and talking at the top of that stairwell. To suggest the same with Saidey seemed to beg the fates for a curse.

What was the last thing Kelly Joe had said to me? "It's like you don't want to," she was talking about getting married. "If you were actually excited, you'd be doing more. It just makes me think we shouldn't even be doing this." I wasn't sure what else to do: the planning was done. I was already coordinating the tux rentals, my groomsmen were all accounted for, I was managing the RSVP & invitation list with her mom, I had *made* us a guest book. After seeing Wedding Guest Books on sale at Walmart for fifty bucks, I went to Michaels across the street, grabbed a cherry red notebook and some sunburst orange silk flowers (matched to our chosen event colors), and hot-glued the flowers onto the cover. It was better than the generic bullshit I had seen, and it cost me a grand total of twelve dollars… as an example of some of the budget details I was involved in.

I had also gone all out on the proposal – had done it at the curtain call for her Senior Recital. She wanted our friends and her family around… her recital was the only time her grandmother, brother, sister, and both parents were all in town together to support her, and all our mutual friends were attending the recital. It had been perfect – I even busted my ass to find the ring locally so I'd have it in time. That was back in November, and it happened in a whirlwind during some of the nastiest fights we'd yet had. What a bittersweet affair. I shook those thoughts away.

Maybe Kelly Joe was right: maybe I wasn't excited to make her the center of everything for the rest of my life. Not that I didn't care for her, but I had grown distant. Hindsight being twenty-twenty, I can see that her tactic, whether conscious or not, was to put me down while I lifted her up. In that way, much energy had already been exhausted to please her. But still, the criticisms came.

Nothing I did was ever good enough because I was never what Kelly Joe wanted. The only time it ever felt easy with her, in fact, was when we were back in Wyoming with her family, and when I thought back to our very first weekend together... much of which also involved late night wanderings on campus.

Back in the present moment, I decided I didn't want to see the grand staircase on my night out with Saidey. Instead, we turned right, moving a few feet north to the smaller theater's entrance. Gently, I worked my master key into the slot of the big beige metal doors that barred passage to the Joe C. Greene Theater. Saidey caught my eye; she was looking at me with anticipation. I grinned, forgetting all about Kelly Joe's bullshit. Slowly, I pulled the door wide, and Saidey slipped into the theater. I followed, careful to catch the door so it didn't slam behind us. I eased it shut, and we were plunged into darkness.

"I can't see," she whispered, sticking close to me.

"It's all good," I reassured. "I know this place like the back of my hand." I led her through the tiny lobby and cautioned her to watch her step because the stairs were awkward and shallow, each one housing a full row of theater seats arranged in a shallow stadium sprawl[4].

She lingered near as we made our way down to the lip of the stage, which was technically part of the building's 'basement' level. The back wall of the theater was but a gaping maw that swallowed light like a black hole. The old shop, where Saidey and I had met, was back there, in that void. The back wall of the Joe C. was actually two enormous sliding doors, and the scene shop sat just behind it. It made loading in

---

[4] It was so shallow, in fact, that one had to be careful not to set a comfortable stride upon descending, else they would certainly lose their footing and topple end-over-end.

impressively sized set pieces easy, and dazzled audiences as they pondered the secret to our spectacles. Nearly a century of performance history, and the University was gutting it all. Danny had told me. They were going to demolish the theaters and restore the building's original design, which hadn't included my beloved venues. The shop, both theaters, the dressing rooms… and my art and memories with it…

"Cool, yeah, I know where we are," Saidey affirmed, peering down into the vacant shop. "It's so empty," she said, a note of sadness in her voice.

"I know," I said in a hushed tone, as though we were at the foot of a grave, "it's been surprisingly hard to have to help. It feels like… burying a friend." I shrugged.

"You have much experience with that," she asked.

"Unfortunately, I do," I said softly. It was true – I'd lost a childhood friend just a few years prior to cancer, not to mention teenage years spent losing family elders. "This place has been home for six years. I love it."

Those eyes of hers caught the green light of the 'Exit' sign off stage right, where only a year prior, I had taken my pre-curtain places as the despicable, boy-buggering poet rockstar, Lord George Byron. Nervously, I'd pace there, listening to the first three pages or so for my entrance cue. It was a role for a rockstar, and I had poured every waking moment into replicating Byron: a posh accent, longer hair so I could curl it into a Romantic Period pompadour. How boisterous – how exhilarating. The preshow jitters it gave me, though, were a nightmare. No matter my confidence, my right leg would loosen up, and the knee would either buckle or give out as the whole thing trembled with anxiety, luffing in my pants like a sail struggling in a gale. That little corridor had been a sanctuary, and now its green light seemed to lead the way to Saidey's heart.

"How do we get to the bigger theater from here?"

"This way. Watch the step down." I reached out and she

took my hand for the help. I turned to our right, where a little foyer housed lockers for the shop assistants. They were tucked under the bottom of the stage left staircase. There were backstage stairwells flanking either side of the theaters, and the dressing rooms and green room existed just behind all that, a half-story above us.

"Wait," Saidey held onto my hand, and it anchored me where she was. Like a rubber band, I sprang back to her, unwilling to let go. She didn't let go either and when I turned, our faces were close.

"What's wrong," I asked.

She was smiling, but there was a tiny nervousness I thought I detected. "It's darker back here. I can't see," she whispered with a laugh.

"Oh, right," I said. "I didn't think of that, sorry."

That nasty monkey voice crept into the back of my head, the same one who had criticized Shylock's innocent failure to make a move.

'Kiss her!' The monkey chattered. 'What are you doing? She's right in front of you and this entire situation *screams* romance. Plus,' he reasoned, 'these buildings will be *gone* in a year or two.' It was true. How lovely – how divine – to have one last secret to share – just Saidey, me, and the ghosts.

A lump slowly formed in my throat. It felt like a stone, but I knew it was guilt. I squeezed Saidey's hand, though. I didn't want to let go. "I can lead us," I reassured. It was true – I had always been adept at seeing in the dark, despite terrible near-sightedness, and I had six years of intimate experience in every veiled nook and cranny of that tired old building.

We giggled giddily up the stairs, though I was careful not to hustle, as was often my inclination. Up we climbed, into the black veil that seemed to envelop the windowless stairwell on Level Two.

I had my key ready.

As I inserted it, I said a silent prayer to the resident ghost:

'Please leave us alone while we're in here,' my inner voice prayed. 'Remember I'm your friend, Alice.'

I was careful not to let the door slam as I ushered Saidey into the musty, cavernous house of the Saint Eva Theater. Its mustard upholstered interior seemed subdued by the golden glare of the lonely ghost light sitting downstage.

"What's the light for?" She was pointing at the ghost light.

"That's the ghost light. Nobody showed you a ghost light this year?"

She shook her head. "Nope."

"It's one of my favorite theater traditions," I said.

"Is it supposed to flicker if a ghost is around or something?"

"Not quite. I mean, this one does, but that's because…" I made my eyebrows hop discretely rather than say the name of our resident stage ghost.

"Because of Alice."

Reflexively, I cringed when she said it out loud. I didn't want to stir up Alice – I could already feel her watching. She'd watched Kelly Joe and I through our first interactions, but we'd been right there backstage where we belonged – in a show that had already been blessed by Alice the full torso apparition.

How would she behave tonight, I pondered internally.

I wanted to have the darkness alone with Saidey.

She shook her head at me, but it wasn't demeaning, like I was used to. It was just playful, with a hint of admiration, I daresay. It helped that she was grinning at me like I was a little boy. I was wise enough to know that was a good thing at this stage of the game.

"So, what does it do?" Saidey pointed at the ghost light up on stage. "You never finished." She wasn't whispering, but she was talking low, just for me. The ghost light's brushed aluminum stand was pale against the warm glow of its caged incandescent bulb. It stood there before the worn black paint of the deck like a lonely Hamlet who'd forgotten whether or not 'to be.'

"Well, the practical use is for whoever comes in first – usually the stage manager or house manager – to see around until they can get more lights on without falling off the edge of the stage. It goes back at least to the days of gas lamps, when they'd have to leave footlights burning to relieve pressure on the valves. No one is in the theater overnight–"

"Except maybe us," she prodded, leaning closer to me.

I laughed. "Yeah, except maybe a couple of creeps. But usually, it's just the ghosts in the theater at night. I can see some wise-ass actor such as myself making a quip of it, y'know? 'Who are ye' leaving the lamps on for, the ghosts,' they challenge the stage manager, then it becomes a thing with the whole cast, then, nearly two hundred years later… here we are."

"Here we are," she said with a shrug.

I may not be many things, my friends, but I am good at detecting the lingering expectations of a kiss. No matter how many times I play our moment back, I can feel that expectation there, in that fleeting moment between us. Our faces were close, her eyes were locked on mine. They shimmered with playful expectation. If I wanted, she seemed to signal telepathically, I was more than welcome to kiss her.

4. ALL THE SMALL THINGS

"Do you want me to switch on the house lights," I offered, pointing up on stage where I knew the breakers were. I didn't want her to be weirded out if we were just friends. Plus, I suspected her answer might clue me in to her intentions. Finding myself alone with her there, I was nervous. Anxiety threatened to rattle me, knocking my knees together. That, I was able to prevent… for the moment.

Saidey's grin pushed her rosy cheeks up, and her eyes sparkled above them like miniature moons over the red mounds of Mars. "No, this is good." She slid into Aisle F and sat down near the center of the row.

I followed her. We sat there for a second, settling into the tired old upholstery of the Eva's seats. I fought my nerves, realizing that coming to a point of rest would only spark physical reactions. I wanted it so bad – nothing dirty – I wasn't thinking about the late hour or the nature of Saidey's text, which did indeed feel like a booty call now that I was with her… alone… in person. But I wanted to kiss… to know she felt the same way – to know she felt close to me.

It had been right there. Why the hell did I ask about the

lights? I was trying to be a gentleman, to make sure I wasn't just projecting my desires onto the situation. The thought of making a move and having her stop me had kept me up at night for weeks. Yet here I was, getting every possible sign and I couldn't bring myself to *act.*

Thou hellish fiend, thou chicken shit,
can you no composure keep?
Kiss the girl, get on with it!
The ghosts herein won't make a peep.

Our hoodies smelled of must and Mary Jane, and the ghost light cast wild barbs of luminosity over her pink pigtails. As much as I liked sitting close, I would have rather been facing her, rapt by the mischief in her cherub-like face. Then, I told myself, I'd forget all about the nasty brambles tangled up in my doomed impending marriage. I'd finally surrender to life with reckless abandon. I'd finally cut loose and live a little.

Saidey had, in our fleeting time together, taught me how to live in the moment… I never had a good habit of doing so, even with the encouragement of our mutual friend, cannabis. For instance, one of my most obnoxious early habits when puffed up on bud was to stand behind the couch, where the kitchen and living room spilled into each other, and I'd snap my head back over to the clock on the microwave. "You guys don't even understand," I would tell Eric and Big Jay when we had the herbs out, "I'm time-travelling." It is, quite possibly, my obsession with Death cutting my adventures short, though it was a far more suppressed fear back in those days.

Two weeks prior, during Shylock's date with Mary Jane, Saidey and I had had a moment while the guest of honor was fumbling around for snacks in the kitchen upstairs. From inside my vintage Teenage Mutant Ninja Turtles sleeping bag, she traced the hard lines of the characters.

"I like the style of this artwork," she admired. Her finger

was on Raphael's cheek.

"Whoa," I said as something struck me.

"What," she pried.

"I just realized our connection to this sleeping bag," I said.

"Oh?"

"The actor who voiced Raphael there," I nodded to the turtle with the red bandana, the one she was tickling, "was Rob Paulsen. His voice was prominently featured in *Animaniacs:* he's Pinky's voice in *Pinky and the Brain.*"

"How do you know this stuff," she marveled, considering the sleeping bag art some more.

I shrugged. "I've always enjoyed those connections between performers and their various roles," I admitted. "Ever since I was a kid."

She nodded.

"Do you have Netflix," I asked her.

"Yeah," she said.

"Did you happen to see the Norwegian film *Troll Hunter*[5] when it was on there earlier this spring?"

"No."

"You should check it out," I said, "but be warned: the actress in it who plays the sound girl is your Norwegian doppelganger. It was spooky. I had to look her up on IMDB to make sure it wasn't secretly you," I teased her.

"Yeah," she said, "I'm secretly a film star in Norway. You caught me!" We laughed, but I meant it.

Watching that film in March had rattled me. I found the actor playing the sound girl attractive, but I couldn't figure out why she seemed familiar to me until halfway through the movie. *She looks like your co-worker,* my mind had finally yelped. I spent the rest of that night ignoring those feelings and blushing in the corner while my roommates and I sat rapt by the narrative.

---

[5] Still my favorite of the 'found footage' film genre.

Back in June, Saidey said, "I'll have to check it out, though. Maybe steal this chick's identity."

I nodded, jokingly considering the notion without making a sound.

After a moment, her attention shifted to the shelf of games and trinkets along the wall across from us. "This is a good space to just be," she said. She was staring at Bushel's fiberoptic lamp, its many filament tendrils undulating red, then green, then blue in hue. Saidey stared at it for a while. I stared at her, a stick of incense billowing away in my left hand. Like a skilled camera operator, I would pull the focus of my eyes back to the incense every once in a while, otherwise I risked drilling an angsty hole through Saidey's fair frame.

Remember this moment, my brain instructed. There was nothing else to life but that basement, that Turtles sleeping bag, and the cunning young woman curled up inside it.

"Have you ever found yourself focusing on the tiniest thing when you're high," Saidey asked, shaking me from my rambling thoughts. She was staring at the stick of desert sage incense I had burning, which she'd plucked from its holder atop the circular wooden coffee table.

"I can't say that I have," I replied, "but then, I haven't had much practice."

"Try it," she said. "Especially with how you feel busy-brained, it'll help you slow down." She patted the futon next to her. I leapt to fill the space. "Like, for me," she continued, holding out the stick between us without leaning away, "I don't know why, but I really enjoy watching incense smoke."

As I settled in next to her, she traced the air above the vine of smoke drifting up to the ceiling, showing me the curlicue that formed. "I just find myself staring at the way it curls off in different directions. Here, look."

She waved the incense ever so slightly. In a moment, the smoke trail changed directions, first curling into a tight spiral, then splitting like a double helix of DNA preparing for replication. Saidey wiggled the end of the stick and produced individual little rings.

"Oh," I commented, impressed by the perfect little circles. Gandalf himself couldn't produce a finer ring. The stick waggled loose in Saidey's grip and ruined the effect. She just laughed.

It was infectious.

She leaned into me, holding the incense out and adjusting so we were shoulder-to-shoulder. There we sat quietly, watching the desert sage billow away, off to mask the floorboards above from the chronic reek we permeated.

I admired her tattoo – she had one on her ankle and wanted another one behind her ear.

"Do you have any," she asked.

I did not. "Is there one you would get?"

I divulged my one tattoo desire, but such things are shared in confidence – in a personal conversation. To do so here would be imprudent, but suffice it to say Saidey thought it was rad.

Shy returned, descending the untreated wooden cellar stairs.

"Hey, Shy? Is the Gaming sign still up?" I had intentionally waited until his feet made it to the bottom of the stairs. Without a second thought, he turned and marched back up the stairs. We laughed as we heard him fuss with the rattling doorknob.

"It's here," he confirmed. Saidey and I made eye contact and snickered. Why wouldn't the sign still be there? A silent moment passed. We heard no movement on the stairs. Then, timidly, Shy added, "Do you want it?"

"What," Saidey blurted incredulously.

"Why would I want it," I asked. Saidey and I broke down laughing. We had adopted one of those cardstock paper door hangers as our signal to ourselves that we were smoking. It said 'Don't Come In: I'm GAMING' with some graphic video game designs tossed in. Left behind by Bushel, it had drawn Saidey's attention.

"That should be our code word," she had said to start the night. "When we're at work or out in public, we can say we were 'playing Halo.' That's a game everyone still plays, right?" It was that very night we set the canon for conversations about weed outside the safety of sturdy D1. That dear old townhouse still cradles my best memories of Black Swamp, the second town any of us ever called home.

Next, we all zoned out on our own, and I found myself staring at the copyright on the Ninja Turtles sleeping bag: 1990.

"Wait," I said to no particular conversation. "I just realized something." We were very stoned by then.

"What," Saidey sat up curiously.

"Didn't you say you were born in 1991?"

"That's right," Saidey nodded. Earlier, she had taken a poll of birth years, trying to piece together our age difference.

In my altered state of conscience, I found my next observation sheerly mind-blowing.

"My sleeping bag is older than you," I announced with disbelief.

She inspected the art of the plush bag and noted the printed copyright in the bottom corner. "By one year," she protested.

It made me feel bashful, though I don't know why. We were only four-ish years apart, and there was far less of an intellectual gap. She had ingenuity and cleverness beyond her years, and a taste for the same coming-of-age 1980s films I enjoyed, like *The Breakfast Club* and her favorite, *Ferris Bueller's Day Off.* She was very wise… grounded and thoughtful. She was everything I thought an artist should be, and she always moved with intent, especially the intention to live in the moment.

I loved it.

I loved her.

I scrunched up my nose. "It just makes me feel old."

"Well, don't," Saidey said. "You're still young. Otherwise, we wouldn't be hanging out with you, right Shy?"

Shy chuckled slightly in his stupor and smiled.

Saidey pressed on. "When you compare ages, you sound like Vance." She meant our co-worker, PhD candidate Vance McHale.

"Vance is an excellent dude," I protested.

"Yeah," Saidey nodded, "but he's in too big a hurry to grow up and be the professor. To be done with school."

"He is almost thirty," Shy defended.

"Right, but he's still in college. He's still in his twenties. He's not enjoying those things if he's focused on who he wants to be once he's outta' here. Everyone gets to college and just wants to grow up. That spoils the fun, doesn't it? Why be in a hurry to end your fun?"

We sat silently in consideration. I made sure to nod thoughtfully. I could see her point. She shrugged at our silence. "We only get to do this once… only get to be young once." I yearned to think she might be appealing to me. Marriage was one of those 'grown-up' things…

Saidey averted her gaze, fixing it on her stick of incense again. "Sorry," she said. "I'm just not in a hurry to be done with this phase of life."

"Don't be," I insisted, "you make a good point. This has been one of my best years in Black Swamp, and it's because I've been soaking it all in," I went on. Absentmindedly, I had picked up the pipe to take another hit, but instead just kept gesturing with it as I talked.

"Jerry, it's a pipe, not a talking stick," Saidey interjected.

"Sorry." I felt myself blush as I passed her the pipe, playing it off with a wink. She wasn't wrong, and she was preventing me from bad habits. In the ensuing years, I'd draw on such etiquette at countless networking parties in the entertainment industry.

Another thing I owe her for.

"Anyway," I picked up my thought, "this year, I've only focused on what's right in front of me – on the present moment – because I don't have time to look forward or back."

She smiled and Shy nodded thoughtfully.

I wish I could remember more of those times we shared alone together. I was so painfully immobilized by the things Kelly Joe had filled my head with, so wrapped up in duty and the next phase of life, so full of self-loathing, that I ignored multiple intimacy right-of-ways with Saidey.

I was *convinced* I wasn't good enough. Nearly four years of trying to prove to Kelly Joe that I was worth her time had left me with a damaged confidence. I hadn't yet realized *that* was how Kelly Joe was keeping me around. The more she spurned me, the more I chased her. Of course, looking back makes me want to bang my head off a wall, but then, have I mentioned hindsight's twenty-twenty?

☙ ❧

Back in the Eva on June 1st, I decided it was time to lean in. The energy coming from Saidey was well beyond platonic. Anticipation itself seemed to glimmer on her lips under the eerie caged bulb of the ghost light. Within a millisecond of deciding to take her cue, guilt pounded on my eyelids, seizing my body before I could close the distance between our faces.

I suppressed the butterflies she gave me – and completely lost sight of all the signs Saidey was giving me as my conscience hammered away.

Think of all the people you'd be letting down, I reasoned; perhaps not *my* family – they'd be secretly relieved – but what of all the wedding planning? What of my fiancé's big Wyoming homesteader family, many of whom genuinely loved me? Despite my degree pursuits in the English program, we were both wrapped up in the theater department. We had all the same friends and mentors. Why derail a good thing?

Those were the reasons I hesitated. But the sad truth was that it wasn't a good thing with Kelly Joe, and I couldn't admit it. Before the engagement, we'd fight because she was mad I hadn't proposed. Then, after I had proposed, and amidst my extra efforts in *graduate school*, she'd stir up shit because I wasn't doing enough of the wedding planning, or I seemed like I didn't care or that I wasn't excited. How could I be? Nothing I did was ever good enough.

My heart spasmed in my chest like Poe's telltale fiend, fluttering like an angry dove about to kill itself in an air duct.

My heart was in deep shit with Saidey. I had spent far too much time imagining us together to move her to the 'friend zone,' but kissing her at that moment felt like a point of no return. If I chose it, my future in New York would dissolve because I wasn't really ready to go anyway, and if Saidey kissed me back, there was no way I was going to get over her.

Would she be able to stand me for more than a couple months? If I listened to my gut and broke off my sophomoric engagement, how long before my imperfections would drive Saidey mad? Somehow, I fancied myself lucky that Kelly Joe tolerated me enough to help me navigate social settings with more humility. She said I often made the wrong impression. She said people thought I was selfish… that things I said in insecurity read as arrogance, and she was right, to an extent. But she defanged this old showman, that wicked witch of the west. She got in my head and made me feel worthless without her approval.

I certainly wouldn't have her approval to kiss Saidey.

The moment lingered.

Saidey's eyelashes batted at me once in slow motion.

Before me, the field was wide open, and I had the ball in my possession. But like some panic-stricken rookie quarterback who gets to the pros and forgets he can run; I was paralyzed with fear. My only reaction was to immobilize.

Plus, I warned myself as I considered, who am I to assume she even wants the complications of a relationship with me – a guy who was set to be married in ten weeks? She had her senior year of undergrad ahead of her, and she didn't strike me as being game for long-term commitments.

Who was to say she wanted anything more than a warm body with a decent face for the night? I had no idea, but I was undeniably already attached emotionally.

Fuck it, I thought. That was my sign from the universe; I should go for it.

Something up in the balcony behind us clanged with fury. We both flinched in shock, obliterating the mood.

Dammit!

5. EVEN IF SHE FALLS

I turned and peered up at the balcony.

"What the fuck," Saidey whispered. There was a little fear in her eyes now. At the time, I was stupid enough to think it might be because of ghosts.

I scanned the shadows up on the third-floor ledge that was the Eva's balcony. It had sounded an awful lot like someone opening the doors out in the balcony lobby, up on the third floor. There was never security in the building.

Shit, I thought. What if it was one of my mentors, here to poke around on a sleepless night? I couldn't stand the resulting mistrust at being found out like this. Not only had the theater faculty treated me like one of their own, but they had all celebrated my engagement to Kelly Joe. Everyone in the department knew us.

Saidey and I waited there in silence, but no other sound came rattling down to us. No person came barreling into the space to scold us.

I kept watching the balcony. I had the distinct feeling I was being watched, and I knew why. It was Alice.

"We're fine," Saidey said. I was elated that she wanted to

stay put. She wanted to be in there with me… alone in the dark. I was going to kiss her, no matter what Alice thought.

But there was no doubt in my gut; Alice was with us. I couldn't see her, but I felt the icy chill of her presence manifest, clouding that grand and cavernous hall.

Aren't you engaged to the little blond minstrel, Alice taunted disapprovingly. *What would she say if she saw you in here with this… this ragtag art-punk tomboy?*

The taunting pressed on in my head as I tried to find the moment with Saidey again.

I dare you to do it. Clearly, you want to. But I can't promise I won't tell. Alice cackled in my head next, enjoying herself. She was up on stage – I felt her lingering directly out of my peripheral, hugging stage left.

Go on – do it! See what happens. I dare you!

The spirit's voice was so loud, so prodding and distracting, that my whole body locked up.

My being flexed as one united muscle, restraining every part of me from shouting up on stage: *Shut the fuck up, Alice!*

Another clang up in the balcony made us both jump again. Saidey turned in her seat, eyebrows raising as she glared up at the balcony. Was that a slight eyeroll I detected? That meant she was frustrated that we were being interrupted! Or maybe I just imagined it. I was, after all, obsessed with her face.

"What the hell," she muttered, slumping back in her seat.

She may have even grunted in frustration as she heard the sound… I cannot now say. Perhaps she did, or maybe it was my desire muddling details.

We stared up into the balcony together. Nothing moved in the shadows… and nothing seemed out of place.

It was only then, after she sat up, that I realized just how far she had reclined in her seat. She'd been sinking into it the way teenagers slouched in movie theater seats so they could fool around. My heart ached to touch her flame – to let myself be young and free again.

Even if she falls in love, Alice hissed, *you'd have a wedding to cancel. You'd have hearts to break, even if she falls for you.*

"What d'you think," Saidey asked, settling back into her chair. I stayed perched on the edge of mine, peering around in the theater's darkest corners.

"I don't think it would be faculty or staff this late." I checked my phone: it was a little after two AM. Shoot, I thought, I was going to run out of time with her. Who knew how long she'd wait for me to make a move.

"C'mon," she said, urging me back into my chair. "We're fine."

Oh, how I wish I had listened. How I wish I had sat back, turned to her, and kissed her there in Row F, in our private viewing of the Eva's slow decay, picked over and withering in the summer night like some beached whale carapace – a metaphor for my contribution to the theater program, and an ominous start to my career in that fickle field of entertainment.

Resetting mentally, I prepared again to pounce, but another noise echoed through the balcony and the fly system. Was it the clang of the old pipes or was it someone pressing the panic bar on one of the many industrial doors out in the hallways?

Dammit!

Someone must have seen us come in and was trying to figure out where we disappeared to. Probably suspected something, especially if they saw we were a co-ed duo. It was college at the turn of the twenty-first century; that was always the assumption when two people of opposite genders were out late together…

In fact, I admitted, that's exactly what I hoped we were up to. I'd roamed around out in the halls and stairwells of the university buildings many times, including that November four long years ago with Kelly Joe. We didn't have anywhere to go on our first date, and we didn't know each other that well, so we walked all over campus, eventually sitting on the big marble staircase outside the Saint Eva. There, we spent hours comparing notes about our family structures, which were shockingly similar – eerily so, in fact.

My father was one of three boys and five girls among his siblings; Kelly Joe's was one of five boys and three girls among his siblings. Neither of our immediate families got along with dad's big family. Our mothers were both born in 1962 and were both the oldest of three children. They both had two younger brothers and a mother still alive, and our families tended to gravitate towards them for holidays. Her maternal grandad had died of cancer a few years back, and mine had just beat lymphoma[6]. On and on, the comparisons went. That had been so long ago – back before I felt worthless. Back when I felt like Kelly Joe was a fool for not being interested in me… because she wasn't.

After our first two dates, she broke up with me right before a big ghost hunting trip to Parma with a bunch of the musical theater kids. She did it again over winter break, just a month after we got together. I shook Kelly Joe from my head, catapulted back to the present in milliseconds…

Back on June 1st, it was just after two in the morning. Next to me, Saidey smirked and leaned in, whispering, "So, how long do we wait?" It felt like another opening. That tiny voice of destiny in the back of my head threw a tantrum at me for not just leaning in.

Another clang behind us, out in the main hallway, rattled off the marble stairs and shattered my nerves beyond recovery.

Saidey nearly launched from her seat, jumping with a start.

Dammit!

Alice hissed in my conscience, chilling the meat around my bones. *You have no plans for living in town longer, even if she says she'll be yours. And what of the money?* She sang that thought like a sad song. *Both your families have spent big for this. I wish I had been*

[6] For one more month, my maternal grandfather was also still alive. He passed at the start of winter break, only four weeks after this memory.

so lucky. Alice clicked her teeth – they clinked like ice cubes in a frosted glass, chilled by her lifeless aura.

Even if she falls in love, she'll get sick of you, just like they all do. She'll reject you, too, even if she falls for you. There's a storm behind your playful eyes. I've watched you – I *can see your soul. You are troubled, and you drive young women away. Not intentionally. But the closer you get to someone, the less their opinion matters. You seek validation elsewhere once you've won a heart. Yes,* Alice hissed, *I've known boys like you.*

Half your mentors here will lose all respect for you in the process, even if she falls in love. Are you prepared for that? Is one night defiling my home *worth all that? Because in the end, that's all you'll be left with. Nothing good will come of this union. I curse you both, like dear Willie's star-crossed lovers.*

I don't believe Alice had actually encountered 'Willie' the Bard in the next realm. She just wanted me to feel small.

"You wanna' go check out the balcony," I fumbled. "Might be a good idea to make sure no one's actually following us." If I could see the whole theater spread out before us, maybe I'd feel more confident that the noises were just Alice, and not someone more… material.

"Sure," Saidey agreed. "If we get caught here because you have those keys *and* you're with an undergrad," she clicked her tongue against her teeth in mock disapproval. "I don't want to get you in trouble."

"A little trouble is fine," I admitted, scrambling desperately to maintain the flirtatious mood. "But maybe not *that* much trouble, yeah."

With that, we stood, situated ourselves, and crept to the back of the house. The smell of aging teakwood clung to us as we clung to the shadows of the little oval-shaped lobby. I cracked the metal fire doors just a hair, listening for anyone out in the cavernous echoes of the marble and plaster-adorned U-Hall chambers.

The coast was clear, so we crept out of the theater and over to the northeast stairwell. From there, we headed up to the third floor, and, slinking like cat burglars, we keyed into the Eva's balcony level. Carefully, I guided Saidey through the entryway, which traced the outer edges of the oval-shaped main lobby on Floor Two below. The balcony lobby's center was open so it could overlook a grand piece of mid-century abstract art installed in the center of the room. We crept over a few discarded ellipsoidal stage lights, slipped up three steps and through the doorway into the balcony's seating section. It was extremely dark inside, but Saidey didn't go for the seats this time. Instead, she walked all the way down to the ledge and took it all in.

The ghost light winked at us from its post down-center. *I'll keep Alice at bay*, it seemed to offer me. I smiled at my inanimate old friend.

"What a great view," Saidey admired.

"I love this place," I blurted, mesmerized by the flicker of that light's lonely, heated filament.

"How do you feel about the new building," she asked sweetly, concern ringing in her voice.

"It's nice," I tried to stay positive. I didn't want her to think I was a constant downer… even though I was pretty sure I *was* a constant downer. Her eyes invited me to share my heart a little more, so I went on. "Everyone wants new facilities. Danny definitely needs them. So does the film department. But I guess I feel like I got to make my mark *here*," I held out my arms, indicating the ground around us with my fingers. "And it was something I was going to leave behind. Last year, especially, I had some killer characters downstairs in the Joe C., and they'll never use those production photos to showcase the department." I shrugged. "I don't mean that to be vain, either. It was a way to outlast my time here – to be worthy of the department's bragging rights, y'know? Because that's what got *me* out here. There was a folder with all the course info, and it was this full-color showcase of different performances and film shoots. I came in with the goal of making it into some of those photos, because it meant I was involved. It meant I was helping to make projects happen here. And instead, it's like none of it matters. All the little marks I've left in here are getting gutted. It's like my work didn't mean anything."

She smiled. "That doesn't sound vain… you care about your work. With a live performance, you don't leave much behind outside of memories. The legacy of your art here feels overlooked. And, to lose this," she nodded at the theater around us. "I can see why it's sad."

"It's really sad," I jumped in. "And it hurts – I get that sinking feeling in my chest, like something with wings is dying in my ribcage…" I trailed off.

"It's okay. I get it." She closed the distance between us and bumped into my side playfully. But the Bard went muttering on in self-reflecting pity instead of taking his cherub's cue.

"I liked learning in older buildings. They have their own history – the performance space does. When you stand down there, you can feel generations of performers learning before you. Their signatures are still on the walls. It's how theater should feel, I think. We're passing down this tradition through generations – thousands of years – hell, we were memorizing shit and keeping track of it way before we were counting years on a Julian calendar. When you're here, learning about that, and then you step out into the lights down there, in front of people, that energy either grounds you in your scene and you harness it – you project it out here for the people… *or* it scares you shitless and you lock up… you freeze, and the audience loses you in a sea of other energy. Put up or shut up… it was perfect."

She held my gaze as I finished, and I met her eyes for a reaction. In them, the reflection of the ghost light gleamed at me from our spot in the balcony.

Thankfully, I couldn't hear Alice anymore, but her questions still burned in my brain.

I graduate in a month, my mind prodded my heart. Even if she falls in love, what's my plan? Everyone else I care about thinks I'm moving to New York City with Kelly Joe. I have no job here – no prospects, no plans. I have nowhere lined up to live, though I could probably figure that out rather hastily. How many friendships do I risk torching if I leap for Saidey?

Go, I now cry to my past self, knowing the torment that was ahead with Kelly Joe. Back then, though, in those moments, I couldn't admit the thorns on her rose of having poisonous buds. I only worried I was already well on my way to hurting her… and Kelly Joe put up with me.

I wasn't sure Saidey would. She was so free – so independent – that I worried we would clash. Now I realize it would have been the healthier choice – the better choice for me. But I had a pattern, and it thrived on codependent relationships. Independence intimidated my heart…

The silence that lingered felt awkward as I realized I'd been rambling about myself. If she wanted a kiss then, I cannot say I would have noticed.

"Sorry," I said sincerely. "I don't think I've dealt with my feelings yet. Seeing it empty like this – gutting it last week…" I shook my head. That had turned into a spiral – I didn't want her to see that. There were far too many soap boxes in my repertoire – they liked to spring out underneath me when certain topics arose. "I don't mean to ruin the mood."

Saidey laughed awkwardly at how I phrased that. Fair enough. "You don't have to apologize. At least you talk about your feelings," she said.

I shrugged. "I'm a sensitive person, I'll admit it. What artist isn't, though?"

"I know plenty," she shot back. That had stirred something up in her. A past relationship, perhaps?

As I let her statement simmer, I realized how right she was. "There's no truer sign of weakness than the inability to admit one's faults… which is probably why most humans are incapable of doing just that."

"That sounds like Nietzsche."

"Nope. Just *Me*-tzsche," I said.

She bleated out a little laugh, but stifled it, recovering with "You're such a dork."

"We've been through this," I corrected. "Geek, please. Show some respect. Dorks are a whole different breed." We had, indeed, been through my observed nuances of the nerd-geek-dork trifecta of social stigmas during Shylock's date with Mary Jane. He was very quiet… Saidey and I did most of the talking. In fact, I reminded myself, that night it felt like she had also been waiting for the chance to socialize with me outside of work.

She was still giggling, so I just kept going. It's a long-standing habit of mine "You're lucky I'm not a dork, actually. Otherwise, this whole situation would be *way* more awkward."

"Oh, yeah," she asked as she chuckled, egging me on. My heart sang when she did that. I wondered if she realized she had good improv technique. She always had a 'Yes, and.'

"Yeah… uncomfortable, even," I went on. "If I were a dork, I might try to kiss you." In the moment, I thought I was testing the waters with a careful suggestion, but hindsight hurts far worse, and that remark sounded like I just put her in my friend-zone.

Dammit, no!

6. DAMMIT

"Oh, really," she said, raising an eyebrow. It felt like a flirtatious challenge, but there was also a chance she had taken it the wrong way.

Shit!

'Unless I didn't misread the situation,' was the romantic recovery line I wanted to use. My brain urged my mouth to speak the words, but I was frozen. There was no way I could be that forward… that direct.

But why not?

Because it made me feel guilty to even think about.

Dammit!

Alice cackled at me from the shadows.

The Man in Tan was quiet… had been for some time. In fact, I had my doubts about him. But Alice was very real. I had felt Alice, had been in the little theater in December when she pushed three twelve-foot pipes over. They nearly hit three of our freshman performers.

I shivered as realization doused me like a cold shower: Alice didn't want me here with Saidey. Alice preferred Kelly Joe – the theater girl.

With that, I coaxed Saidey back towards the shadows in the little hallway connecting the balcony level to the lobby. We lingered at the threshold to the balcony lobby. I leaned in. The wings of my heart fluttered under my ribs like the Mad Hatter's steaming ears on his very merry un-Birthday. I took a sharp breath as I leaned close.

The doors below on Floor 2 creaked open an inch.

Dammit!

We both jumped back against the carpeted walls, and I shifted into action without a second thought. "Follow me," I whispered. Out the lobby doors we ducked, into the third-floor hallway. I waved her with me to the right, towards the north stairwell (at the top of the '+'), then down to Floor 1 as swiftly as we could go. Out to the covered pedestrian walkway we fled, then I turned left, and we shot out of the walkway. As we exposed ourselves to the brisk night breeze, I steadied my pace. No need to look like we were fleeing. We followed the sidewalk north across University Lawn, keeping U-Hall's neighbor, Hannah Hall, to our right. I had done this because the theaters extended east off the back of the grand building, so if someone was following from the theaters, they would have a very, very slim chance of spotting us.

To further dispel inconspicuousness, we circumnavigated Hannah, through the center 'loop' of Black Swamp U, and I forged a path to the science buildings up north. As I may have mentioned, I had a working knowledge of which buildings stayed unlocked all night. That was a result of previous expeditions – not with young women, but often alone. I was either location scouting or trying to spark my imagination or trying not to think about a girl.

College had been one missed opportunity after another, but none of it mattered. I didn't want those opportunities – I just wanted the present night – June 1st, 2012 – with Saidey. Romantic expression of some kind, and all the heartache and angst of college monogamy would evaporate because it was all baseless and dumb, and what I felt for Saidey was frighteningly real. I wanted to change my life to be with her. I was ready to rip the tablecloth out from under the fine Rocky Mountain China I kept prancing around gingerly.

"Have you ever been to the planetarium," I asked.

"No," she said. "I took that 'Intro to Astronomy' class freshman year, but the class met in a lecture hall."

"What," I gasped. "Oh, no. I had that class inside the planetarium… at like four-thirty, which was right after my only break for dinner three days a week. I'd order a sandwich at the Union food court on my way, then I'd devour it on a bench out here," I pointed as we rounded the corner, passing my old benches. "Then I'd go to class and sit back in those plush chairs… add a food coma and oof!" I rubbed my stomach.

Saidey laughed. "How did you ever pass," she teased.

"Funny story," I shot back. "I stopped going to class."

"What? How does that work?"

"The class got *real* basic. Either people weren't responsive, or the public school system is failing[7]." I squeezed the bridge of my nose, exaggerating my frustration. "The teacher was reduced to basic atomic science: protons, neutrons, electrons, and how they form elements and react with each other."

Saidey scrunched up her face. "I learned that in, like, sixth grade," she protested.

I nodded in agreement, stopping just outside the doors. "But the teacher only took attendance by randomly giving quizzes. Every other big test question was in a series of online quizzes that we could take like eight times to learn the facts. She'd set the in-person quizzes in the little foyer leading to the planetarium, so I'd wait for class to start, cut through the lobby to the men's room, and look for the stool with the tests on it. If I didn't see a test, I went back to the dorms and played sci-fi video games instead. Usually, things in outer space… I felt it

---

[7] Little did I realize…

necessary to at least stay on-topic."

Saidey shook her head in disbelief at some unseen realization. "Save Ferris," she said.

"What," I chuckled.

"Your tactic reeks of Ferris Bueller," she said.

My heart melted. That was a true compliment, especially coming from the girl with the Ferris Bueller shirt. Even though she liked Cameron more than Ferris.

Fuck.

Or… did it matter? Ferris Bueller was cool. If she was comparing me to him, did that mean she thought I was cool? At least to some extent? It was a status I'd sought my whole life. 'Cool' had eluded me through adolescence, and I still wasn't sure I had the slightest idea what 'cool' looked like.

Saidey's smile was wicked under the ghostly amber streetlight at that far corner of campus. No wonder she always wore her cap, I thought. It was far too easy to look into her soul with eyes as bright and clear as a cloudless day.

"I told you 'Ferris Bueller' was my nickname at my undergrad job, didn't I," I rambled on. "My professor's the one who gave it to me after a conversation kind of like this one."

Saidey grinned, shaking her head at me. "I can see that. It suits you." Her smile sank daggers into my heart.

"Astronomy was nothing," I went on. "In Biology 101, the teacher took attendance with these stupid little digit pad remote control things," I explained.

"Oh, yeah! I had those for a science class, too."

"Pain in the ass, those things. But my buddy Cole and I would sit in the very back, on the aisle. We'd keep things light, sometimes not even bring a bag, and we'd take attendance on the remote controls. Then, maybe fifteen or twenty minutes in, once we were sure there wasn't a quiz, one of us would go to the 'restroom' – taking all belongings, of course – then duck outside of the building and wait for the other. We'd walk back to our dorm together and do something else… anything else.

Usually video games."

Saidey nodded in agreement, adding a cheeky half-shrug.

"The teacher uploaded all the slides online, and the tests were all based on the slides. All we had to do was attend lab once a week, print the slides for tests, and pass those tests. Plus, the occasional class where attendance was a quiz halfway through the lecture."

"Yeah, but what was your final grade," Saidey challenged, clearly ready to laugh at me.

"Three-point-two," I gleamed.

"Oh, okay. So, your method worked?"

"Oh, yeah," I said. "I'm the king of skirting by," I shrugged. "My parents thought I could have done better in high school if I had focused more," I confessed. "But it always felt like I had to constantly be working to keep up with those top-twenty kids, and I just cared more about life – about getting better at the things I wanted to be doing. Plus, I graduated with a three-point-six, and I was ranked in the top twenty-five-percentile, so what's the point of applying yourself *more* and missing out on living? Having a girlfriend and a favorite band… time out with friends. High school should be about those things, too. What *youth* should be about. Instead, we make it about careers and money and all that bullshit."

I stopped, holding the door to the science building open for her. If I'm being honest, I was probably Goldbluming[8] at this point.

"Such a gentleman," she curtsied.

I couldn't help but notice how cute her backside was in her little checkered shorts. "Just being polite," I said. "I know you're perfectly capable." I was being sincere.

"Don't apologize for that." Then, somewhat timidly, she

---

[8] 'Goldbluming' is the term my closest friends have coined for those instances when I channel one of my Pittsburgh actor heroes. It was a combination of thoughtful gesticulations and easy, rolling vocals of eccentricity that made me sound far too much like Jeff Goldblum.

added, "I like that you do that."

I shrugged. "It ruffles some peoples' feathers."

"That says more about them, I think. And fuck them, anyway!"

I leaned in to kiss her, but I had already opened the second set of doors without thinking, and she slipped through without realizing we were having another moment.

Dammit!

Once inside, we checked the planetarium… if it was open, it was an even darker, more secluded spot than the Eva. Anticipation writhed in my chest like a dying worm as I reached out to test the metal double doors. They were locked.

Dammit!

Saidey pressed her face and hands to the glass, peering into the dark, domed room. "I can see those seats you're talking about. So plush."

"They're pretty great," I affirmed.

She met my eyes, those icicle blue orbs of hers freezing me to the tiled floor. I had no idea where to take her to be in private. So many missed opportunities… I cussed myself internally. Saidey and I existed in our own little bubble for the night, and the energy in that bubble screamed at me to kiss her. It was deafening, and I was so painfully uncertain… that, and ensnared in an emotionally antagonizing engagement.

I shrugged, shaking those tangled snares, and scanned the cramped science building's hospital-like lobby. There was a stairwell back by the restrooms. I wandered over into the shadows of that corner and tried the doors on a whim. They clicked as they unlatched. The dark stairwell beckoned me.

"You ever been in this building," I asked.

"I don't think so," she said with a smile.

"And I've only ever seen the first floor," I offered. "That's a lot of undiscovered country…" I paused, taking a dramatic beat and raising my eyebrow. "They could be up to anything way over here on the edge of campus… with their *science.*" I used a debonair 1940s silver screen dialect – it was somewhere between Humphrey Bogart and Gregory Peck.

Saidey raised a suspicious eyebrow, playing along. "Someone has to hold them accountable," she warned. Her cheeks bloomed whenever she did something silly or performative, almost like she was embarrassing herself in the process. It was perfect. There was just something about the way her fair, strong cheeks so divinely framed her eyes when she grinned or laughed or smiled… when she was having fun… when *we* were having fun together.

"We haven't a moment to waste, Pinky." I channeled Maurice LaMarche channeling Orson Welles.

"You're way too good at that," Saidey teased with feigned wariness.

I held the door wide and gestured politely for her to go first. Into the bleak, dark stairwell we went. The shadows were extra grey, like all our light was being filtered through cobwebs. It was the effect of worn-out fluorescent tube lights on a nighttime dimmer.

The first two floors were locked up and we couldn't get in. But there were four more floors above us. We kept climbing – the door to floor five was propped open.

"Success," I said in my Brain voice.

We crept quietly up the landing and peeked down the dark hallway. All the rooms were closed, their doors standing sentinel along that narrow, sterile passage. A few doors' windows glowed, casting their sad pale green lumen into the lonely hallway.

As I peered to the right, down another hallway, I spotted a janitor cart parked outside the restrooms. I popped back into the stairwell and signaled for her to stay quiet. Then, I waved her on, and we crossed out of the stairwell, past the janitor's side of the hallway, and kept going straight. That put the corner between us.

Quietly, we made our way to the end of the hallway. There

was another corner. The whole hallway ran around the floor in a square. Around that corner, there was another exit stairwell. None of the rooms were unlocked, for we had quietly tried them all along the way.

In one of the rooms, we spotted some empty cages, no doubt for animal testing. We frowned at each other.

"Lucky for them," I ruminated quietly as Brain, "these cages are empty."

Saidey stifled a laugh.

Why did it feel so good when she laughed at my clowning? It had never felt like that with Kelly Joe. I rammed that thought deep down inside. Back in the moment, there was a hesitation as we locked eyes.

Go! Desire shouted at my body. *That's an opening for a kiss. You missed too many tonight. Go!*

Thump!

Bang!

The janitor's thick plastic pushcart rattled as he exited the restroom.

Dammit!

We both jumped away from each other. That was a good sign, right? That meant she was feeling the kiss in that moment too, which had to mean she wanted me to try and kiss her.

Of course, she does, you absolute buffoon! She's sneaking around campus with you at three in the fucking morning! Now, do like Sebastien the Crab says and 'Kiss thee girl!'

We stood close, listening as the janitor replenished supplies. Their grumbles echoed to us around the corner, along with the tinny grooves from a shitty pair of Walkman headphones. Whoever the deep-voiced grumbler was, he was enjoying the dulcet tones of The Backstreet Boys.

"I never wanna hear you say, I want it that a-way," he sang along with discretion and passion. Saidey and I realized this at the same time, shooting each other questioning glances.

'What the hell is going on,' I mouthed to her, holding back

more laughter.

She let her shoulders slouch and shook her head.

We waited until we heard the groovy janitor enter the other restroom, then Saidey tugged my arm.

She pulled me around the next corner, and we dove into a brand-new exit stairwell. We plunged into darkness as the door shut behind us. Simultaneously, the restroom door opened again as the janitor returned to his cart. "Hey," I heard his belching grumble of a voice call out after us.

"Keep going," I urged quietly. We swung around the handrails, our Vans barely whispering like feathers on the concrete steps.

The door upstairs opened, and I pulled us into a corner two stories directly below that fifth-floor landing.

"Who's there," the janitor honked into the darkness. Hesitation warbled his grumble, and he sounded like a panicked turkey in mid-November.

Saidey's gaze met mine and, as the janitor huffed like a deterred predator and let the door slam shut behind him, we both guffawed silently, convulsing so hard my face ached. It was the bliss of a laugh that must be discreet; a laugh that, because it must be suppressed, floods the body, amping comedic convulsions into maddening bliss.

There was that creeping feeling in my gut every time she looked at me while we laughed. Was it her expectation? I was scared shitless to find out. Each time our eyes found each other in the midst of that innocent joy, the tension clung to the air around us. Those moments reverberate like ominous musical notes echoing at me from the past.

Dammit, man, I cuss my younger self, *your whole life is ahead of you and things with Kelly Joe are dashed against the rocks so hard, you'll barely survive the storm. Bring the boat in, Bysshe!*

Back in the science stairwell, trembles of thunder outside rocked my conscience, and I managed to stifle the rest of my laughter. "C'mon," I nodded, "let's find another floor."

I didn't feel inclined to stay in the hallway. Guilt magnified everything. Somehow, in my mind, being seen by anyone else on campus made our secret harder to keep. Kelly Joe was supposed to be my Black Swamp Sweetheart. Our fates and best memories were supposed to be tied to that sprawling campus.

Did I really have it in me to betray that?

I decided I did. All I wanted was to haunt those same hallowed grounds this and every night with the young woman next to me… but I didn't think she felt as deeply. In fact, I reasoned, I still didn't know for sure that she had feelings for me. Ever the insecure fool! Perhaps now the irony in my frustration with Shylock comes into crisp focus.

God-fucking-damn-ME!

7. UP ALL NIGHT

Another opportunity missed. All the doors were locked on the way down that stairwell, and at the bottom, we spilled out into a weatherized glass walkway – a series of ramps between two science buildings, meant for safe transferring of experiments in the harsh weather.

It was perfectly lit, glowing like an aquarium to those who might walk past outside. When I was a freshman, I had urges to write a science fiction film set in those bright glass halls, but now, I had no interest in lingering. If the stairwell hadn't cut it as a good spot for a kiss, the glass hallways cut it about as well as a pair of plastic safety scissors.

My heart throbbed. Had I let the moment pass already? Was I doomed to spend eternity remembering this emotional limbo?

My mind tried the proverbial 'brush off' and we trudged along. "Have you ever been to the Viscom building?"

"The what," Saidey asked.

"It's open twenty-four hours because they have Adobe and Final Cut in the computer labs there."

"What does Viscom even mean?"

"Visual Communication Technologies," I said. "Big Jay is a Viscom grad."

"Oh, so, like, the graphic design school," she said.

"Yeah," I said. "And my other buddy went through the program, but his focus was on physical printing techniques, like screen-printing for t-shirts."

"Oh, cool."

We wandered over that way quickly, up to the north end of campus. The only thing beyond us was the little bi-plane airstrip because the University had some exclusive boutique aviation program, too. Some nights, the Viscom building was lit up like a hotel, but at that hour of that summer night, everything was locked. The university was between spring and summer semesters for one more week, so those facilities didn't need to be accessible.

"It's okay," Saidey encouraged. "Let's go somewhere to pack the pipe again."

Yes ma'am, I thought. We'll go to The Hill.

The Hill was simply that: the only hill on campus. It was not natural, as it was the same shape and size as a bulldozer cleft in a new housing development. I never bothered to point this out to my Ohioan friends. The horizon is lonely out their way. But The Hill had a nice little crop of trees against its southwest ramparts, which was only a dozen paces or so northeast of the Viscom building.

"We can be like the stoners from my adolescence," I teased her, pointing to the trees.

"How?"

"Have you ever been to Pittsburgh?"

"Nope. Seen pictures. There are lots of bridges, right?"

"Yeah," I beamed, "and everything is just built into and up the sides of the Appalachian Mountains. Trees everywhere, too. Probably not as many as when I was growing up, but there's a lot to break up the skyline. "Anyway, the teenagers in the neighborhood would hide out in the woods between everyone's backyards and get high. Sometimes, you could smell it from our back porch."

We pulled up under the not-so-impressive trees, and Saidey produced the pipe and her lighter from the pocket of her hoodie and then produced a plastic baggie with more pre-ground flower. She repacked the bowl and took the first hit.

"My mom even warned me to 'stay away' if I ever smelled it while I was spending time outside."

Saidey laughed and passed the smoking pipe. "'Stay away,' Like you're avoiding a bear or something!"

We cackled together. I paused to take my hit. "But now," I said, setting up another joke, "I know better. It's like Blue Oyster Cult said, 'Don't fear the reefer.'"

Her smile was wonderful. "Oh, yeah? Is that what they said?"

The bats and birds in my heart sang together as she kept laughing. I wanted to make eye contact so I could kiss her, but I couldn't find the moment. I stopped looking, unwilling to force it.

Instead, I sat in the moment. The air had shifted since I picked Saidey up. Instead of the persistent moisture of summer humidity, the night sky, though clear and starry in many patches, was also spotted with wispy grey nighttime rain clouds. The air smelled of peat moss and well water, telltale signs of an impending summer shower in the swamp.

"Smells like rain," I said quietly, almost to myself.

Saidey giggled. "You can smell the rain?"

"Can't you?"

She stopped, her smile slackening into neutral, thoughtful reflection. "No, or… maybe? I don't know."

"It's the way the air smells now," I encouraged. "That mossy, earthy smell? And it's mixed with a… water smell. I don't know how to describe it."

"Water's not supposed to have a smell."

"But the particles in it do. Like when a glass of water sits out for a day or two, and then it has that mineral smell, like standing water."

"I mean," Saidey hesitated, "I definitely smell the earthy part."

"Also," I added gently, "I had noticed the clouds because I was enjoying the night sky."

We each took another hit.

"Did you know that water – pure water – doesn't conduct electricity?"

"Really?"

It's actually the minerals and whatnot present in water that make it such an effective conductor."

"I don't think I've heard that before."

"I distinctly remember the lab experiment in high school."

"Cool," Saidey said. "I think I missed that one."

"You also went to school in Ohio."

"And you're going to *college* in Ohio, you jerk," she teased, punching my arm gently.

"I was just talking about the public schools," I defended playfully.

"A likely story," she said, taking another hit. She peered skyward, nodded in appreciation as she exhaled. "I don't know any constellations," she confessed. "I mean, I know the names of some, but I never learned to pick them out."

"I only know a few," I confessed.

"Really? You seem like the type who'd know 'em all."

"I used up too much brain capacity memorizing film trivia when I was a teenager. All there's room for is The Big and Little Dipper – Ursa Major and Minor – Draco, Scorpius, and Orion, my favorite. But he's not visible this time of year.

"Why Orion?"

I shrugged. "Well, as a kid, I learned about Orion's Belt because of the Men in Black movie with Will Smith. And ever since, Orion has been the easiest for me to spot – even easier than the North Star – and it's just because the movie called attention to it for me. Once I got a little older, I gleaned a basic understanding of astrology, but I can never find Sagittarius – that's my Zodiac," I clarified, "but Orion's always there, shining bright for my birthdays in the winter sky." I shrugged, "If we got to choose a constellation for our Zodiac sign, I'd pick Orion."

She held my gaze for a moment. I couldn't tell what urges stirred behind her eyes. "Sagittarius makes so much sense for you," she said with a nearly undetectable little sigh of admiration.

That was another opening, my mind shouted with glee.

We each took our final hit, sitting together and just existing there at the base of The Hill, forever in that moment of understanding and youthful desire.

As the moment settled and the beasts in my chest urged me closer to her, a heavy raindrop planted itself firmly amidst my arm hairs and burst into wet shrapnel.

Maybe Saidey wouldn't notice.

"Uh oh," she said on cue. "Did you feel that?"

I was not about to lie to her. "Yeah," I said, nodding. "I did. We should head back towards the heart of campus in case it pours."

"Any ideas?"

"There are usually a few buildings open over by The Foxe Center," I offered. "Let's head that way." The new theater building would be completely locked down, and I had no master keys for the spaceship, but I was optimistic the rain would hold. The Foxe was on the opposite end of campus from my car, which bought me more time to make a move before we called it a night. I was already hyperaware of how fleeting my chances were growing as the night waned.

We trekked southeast from there, over to the easternmost edge of campus – out by all the sports facilities and the freshman dormitories where I'd spent my first two years in Black Swamp. It was never as quiet on that side of campus (because of the freshman dorms and the sports events), but at three AM on June's first morning, it was a ghost town. Most of Black Swamp was, but campus *especially* was.

The rain held. It spattered loosely as it chased us out of the northern fields and ushered us back to the heart of campus. Then, it seemed to falter as we passed the cemetery. After a fifteen-minute walk, we sauntered up the grassy incline along the Foxe building's strange spine.

Everyone had taken to calling the new building 'the crashed spaceship.' It had a thin, wedge-like geometry, and the glass-façade at the front, which faced a parking lot in the campus interior, appeared as one might imagine the inexplicable afterburners of some futuristic astro-war machine. They were trying to conserve green space, so the wedge had been proposed to maintain a lawn up its low end. It was strange, and not necessarily inviting. But it was something. In decades past, the lawn would have been ripped up, bulldozed, and paved to make way for the building without any regard for green space.

We sat there quietly on the Foxe Knoll, and I pointed out Polaris and Ursa Major. I was good and stoned, my heart numb to the blunders I faced throughout the night's adventures. Instead, I was happy. Happy to be there. Happy to be with her, and therefore, happy to be me… because I was who Saidey was spending the night with.

I was the guy she'd texted.

I was the guy sitting next to her on that cold concrete slab the Swedish designers insisted was a bench. The pain in my boney ass said otherwise.

"You're fun to hang with," Saidey said as we sat there contemplating the stars. "I like how you think," she added.

"Thanks," I said. "You, too." I grinned at her.

My conscience screamed onto the scene again. Was it private enough up on the ledge of the Foxe Center, just outside of the faculty offices?

With all the glass walls facing the lawn, I had been surprised to learn that there wasn't a security camera in the faculty offices. There were only four points at which security cameras had been installed, and those were all on the northern, western, and southern sides of the crashed spaceship. The wedge of grass comprised the eastern side of the building, considered the back. I knew that, on the other side of all the industrial A/C units and concrete barriers, was our spot. That was where the scene shop's loading dock was; where we had coffee with the crew each morning. It was where she'd greet me each morning, smiling the way she was right now. Of course, I did not call on my knowledge of the cameras that night. Every open window was a chance for more eyeballs to catch me chasing the specters of young love. My skin crawled.

But, I noted optimistically, I did not feel Alice's presence watching us here. No ghosts judging us in the new building. It had just opened in January, had just had its first true semester with students and faculty and staff and performances. It was the new, shiny toy all the art departments were bickering over. The most prominent two undergrad stage managers claimed to have formally invited both Alice and the Man in Tan over to the new building with everyone.

I had also invited Alice – more than once – when things were quiet, and it was just the two of us. I told her I cared – told her how I was mad about losing the old buildings. And I got the sense she was grateful, but in the end, she wasn't going. After all, she had reasoned, she wasn't tied to the brick and mortar or the wood and metal. She was a part of the campus – a part of the legends – a part of Black Swamp mythos. Wouldn't that outlive any demolition? It would let some light in, too, I had noted. Alice hadn't seen daylight in over six decades.

'Leave the ghost light on for me,' I had told Alice. 'When I come back to visit, I'll look for you where the stage should be.'

I wished Alice had remembered those things tonight. How aggravating! I had treated that ghost like a friend for six years. She'd been unfair to me tonight.

Silence between Saidey and me lingered, but it wasn't uncomfortable. Campus was quiet, suspended in time around us. Maybe that's why the rain held, I mused to myself.

In Black Swamp, sometimes the only living thing out that late at night is the angry wind. It sweeps and brushes and hurries people along no matter the time of year, desperately trying to keep the town's sidewalks clean and clear.

Another cloudbank swept in, gloomy charcoal grey fingers that strangled the starlight. I felt awkward, trying to think of what to say to pull her gaze back to me. Could I finally do it?

"This is nice," I said. "I haven't really enjoyed this side of the building much."

"Really? You practically live here."

I shrugged. "No one ever wanted to join me."

"Glad to be the first," she nodded sharply with a smile. Her cheeks bloomed. Then, she yawned.

I hadn't been thinking about the time – hadn't been paying attention, but it had to be late. And we both had work tomorrow… today, technically. We both had to be in the shop – back here in this very building – at seven in the morning.

"What time is it," she asked after her yawn had passed.

I checked my phone. Shit! "It is four thirty-nine," I said, genuinely surprised. I was both disheartened that so much time had passed and thrilled that we could spend so much time together without noticing. What I didn't let myself admit then was that those are tell-tale signs of a budding romance.

"We should probably head back," she said. I could hear the reluctance in her voice, though. "I should get some sleep if I'm gonna' make it to work on time."

"That's fair," I nodded, "me, too."

My demons danced around my mind's fire, taunting me in a ritual to all my missed opportunities. I still had the walk back to the car, I rationalized. That was all the way across campus, and then there was saying goodbye…

I'll spare dragging out the rest. It never happened. My legs buckled every time I thought about it. I wanted to stop walking, grab her hands to stop her with me, and tell her how I felt. I willed myself a million times to do it between the crashed spaceship and the U-hall parking lot.

But every time, Alice hissed her warning; '*Even if she falls*,' she'd remind me, and sure enough, my conscience padlocked my knees, choked out my voice, and scrambled my brain.

Every single time.

We'd take a step, I'd think to stop, hesitating as my mind cried with fear.

ALICE: *If she falls for you tonight,*
Do you have not one real fright
Regarding all the consequence?
DE VERE: *I cannot stand to ride the fence.*
ALICE: *What will you tell your mentors dear?*
DE VERE: *My own family might truly cheer.*
ALICE: *But airline fees, twelve-hundred spent,*
That was four times your monthly rent.
And then there's still that little thing,
blood tied to that engagement ring.
DE VERE: *For years I vied with Kelly's kin,*
To have a spot, to fit within
Their ranks of what I thought was love,
But fled with great haste, did their dove.
They judged, compared, and bickered oft,
However, each held me aloft.
They made me feel adventurous,
And helped me find true wilderness.
How would they act? What would be best?
Could I stand to lose my wild west?
Am I just clinging to the past,

Desp'rate to make the Black Swamp last?
Big Jay was moving out with me,
I could not pass on N-Y-C.
So many things hinged on that night,
My love for her was mental blight.
Or so, that's how it felt right then,
Convinced Saidey had other men
Far better suited to her taste.
I merely served as someone safe.
So, even if she falls in love,
We'd only have one night thereof.
If she falls, it spells disaster,
For, to her I'd cling like plaster.
She'd get tired, spread wings wide.
'We told him so,' the fates would chide,
And then, for years, I'd run and hide.
Alone and broken, I'd reside.
Around, my thoughts did rattle thusly,
And that night brought nothing lusty.
I drove her home; we said good night.
No kiss struck me like dynamite.
It tore me up, I hobbled home,
How next might we find time alone?

I tossed and turned, lying awake in bed from five until a quarter after six, replaying our night over and over again, turning it from side to side like some valuable collector coin, appreciating every groove, every bump, every scuff.

The next day, she didn't show up to work. My heart hurt like a boyhood memory of that first unrequited schoolyard crush. Maybe she couldn't face me? Maybe I embarrassed her by *not* making a move after she had set us up for time alone.

I wanted to see her again before I left for the weekend. Before I had to go play fiancé while a bunch of musicians laughed and drank and sang and made merry around my awkward self. My heart cried out.

I texted to check in on her around eleven, exhausted and thankful that Danny was going to cut us a couple hours early for lack of a to-do list that day. She texted back within ten minutes:

'I'll be in after lunch. Needed some sleep – your fault! ;)'

If only that statement were as suggestive as the tone it was swaddled in. It still felt intimate – it *was* still intimate. We were up practically all night together, and it was our little secret. I tried not to be bummed that she wouldn't be around for lunch break.

After lunch, once Saidey showed up, things were back to normal. Not in the sense that all was well, either. I mean 'back to normal like nothing special happened.' There were no flirty side-eyes or knowing glances, no perfectly rounded porcelain cheeks blushing pink as petunias. Maybe I was just up in my head, but it felt like she was keeping her distance from me. Her distance, her gaze – she seemed private that day.

I was able to snag a moment alone when we both sidled up to the same workbench in the vast and immaculate Foxe Center Scene Shop. Playfully, I gently nudged her. "Hey, you."

"Hey," she seemed to force a smile.

Whoa. My mind shuddered to a halt. What was wrong? Her energy matched that of someone who was trying – and failing – to hide the fact that they were regretting a one-night stand.

Jesus Christ, what did I do?

"Everything okay," I managed to inquire gently, despite the ghastly specter that had wrapped her freezing dead clawed fingers around my Adam's apple. Was it Alice or was it my own conscience choking the moment?

She nodded, smiling weakly. "Yeah, I'm just super tired."

"I thought you were a night owl." I tried to sound playful.

"Yeah, I dunno."

I tried a gentle, "Sorry?"

"Don't be," she said quietly, nudging me back a little. "How many people can say they've done that?"

"Probably more than either of us realizes." I felt my crooked grin hook my left dimple, tugging that edge of my mouth into its mischievous curl.

She grinned. "Don't spoil my fun."

That interaction would have to tie my heart over for another long weekend along Lake Erie's shores, at Cedar Point under Kelly Joe's thumb.

Admittedly, try as I might, all I recall of those weekends now is that I couldn't be with Saidey. Anxiety bubbled as I searched frantically to figure out how and when I'd get another chance to be alone with her.

8. WHAT'S MY AGE AGAIN?

Thank the fates, I did not have to wait long. That Monday, at one of our communal Dunkin lunches with Big Jay, we were discussing the impending release of the summer sci-fi movie, *Prometheus:* the prequel to the *Alien* franchise that director Ridley Scott insisted was not a prequel to his 1979 classic.

"Oh, is that the new sci-fi movie coming out? I kinda' wanted to see that," Saidey chimed in.

"Come with us on Thursday night," Big Jay said with his suave smile. He was single, but he also was more comfortable around girls than most straight men with lean dating histories. It is, I suspect, a symptom of growing up with three sisters. I didn't feel threatened. In fact, I almost hugged him right there. In my mind, it was far more harmless and platonic if Saidey tagged along at his invitation.

"Are you sure? I don't wanna' interrupt 'guys' night' or something."

"Please," I said. "For one, we don't really do 'guys' night' and, more importantly, we're both moving to New York, where we will continue to hang out. You, however, are not, so you better just hang with us while you can."

"Oh, don't say it like that," she interjected with heartfelt protest. As she said it, she and I both glanced reflexively at the empty seat where Shy had, in weeks past, joined us.

"It *is* one of the late showings," Big Jay warned her.

"Good to know," she nodded. "You going to the Small?"

"Yep," I confirmed.

"You can't beat that matinee price," Big Jay admired.

The 'Small' was a dying indoor shopping mall at the very north end of town. Like most things on the edge of town, it was surrounded by crop fields and wild grass that always had that dead, sallow brownish-yellow hue of dying vegetation. A Cinemark and an Eddie Bauer were the main arteries pumping life into the Small. Before our time in Black Swamp, the students around town had lovingly dubbed it the 'Small' to better express its humble presence. Half the shops inside were empty, and the other half of stores still open rotated businesses out every semester.

"We prefer the Small," I affirmed. They premiered movies late on Thursdays but charged the Friday matinee price if it let out after midnight. We saw every new release for a whopping four dollars. The normal ticket price was eight-fifty. In college, that saved us enough to see a movie *and* get some burgers at Rally's in a two-for-three. At that point in our lives, a night of entertainment around town for nine bucks was a godsend.

"Count me in," Saidey said with a satisfied expression on her cherub cheeks as she smiled at me.

"There won't be any more four-dollar movies in New York, that's for sure," Big Jay warned playfully. "We gotta' make the most of it."

Lunch was over, but we were resolved in our plans. My summer classes were in full swing, so the week sped by. I hated leaving the shop in the afternoon – Saidey was there all day until things shut down at four, but I was stuck leaving ninety minutes early for *History of Art & Style* – the theater department's comprehensive but bloated course on the evolution of art over the entirety of human existence.

When Thursday rolled around, Saidey showed up early. Realizing she had also done this for our night with Shylock, I made a mental note. She's coming over to spend more time with you… to be alone with you. The urge to kiss her was extreme, grappled to the ground by my hyperactive conscience.

Unfortunately, shortly after she arrived, my roommate Ash keyed in. Dammit! We retreated up to my room. I left the door half open, not wanting my roommates to suspect anything adulterous. Without hesitation, Saidey sat on the side of the bed.

Edwyn was also due home – half of the basement served as our game room and his bedroom was situated in the other half. The basement was usually where we'd smoke when others were home. Edwyn had been stuck back home in Toledo, I explained to Saidey, so I thought the basement would be free. It wasn't, and I wasn't sure where to smoke discreetly without stinking up the place.

"That's okay," Saidey said. "Do you have any dryer sheets?"

"Yeah, in the hall closet," I confirmed as I stuck my head out of my room and into said closet next door. I plucked two dryer sheets from the box and offered them to her.

"We can make a sploof."

"A what?" Unintentionally, I delivered that question as if channeling Chris Tucker in the *Rush Hour* movies.

She laughed. "A sploof. I did this at home in high school all the time. My mom had no idea." She hesitated, then, "At least, I *think* she had no idea."

She requested a cardboard tube. The toilet paper in the upstairs bathroom was nearly out, so I pulled the paper off and folded it in a frail little stack. I packed the bowl while Saidey constructed the sploof with a flourish of her hands and a tossing of her pink braids.

"So," I asked, "how does it work?"

"You take a hit and exhale into the open end. The smell dissipates when it goes through the dryer sheet. It only masks the smell, though, so if you don't want your room stinking, we could go in the bathroom and turn the fan on."

"Let's do that," I said. Perfect! Close quarters and I doubted Big Jay would arrive early. Work was busy, and they were pumping designs out of him before he left for New York because they liked his style. The university was refurbishing all their old food courts, and there were new buildings and amenities popping up around campus like wildflowers. He wasn't due until seven thirty, and Saidey had shown up around six-twenty. Plus, Big Jay had to get his dinner sorted and we were set for a 9:50 p.m. screening. He knew we couldn't get in line for seats until 9:20, so I suspected he'd take his time.

Saidey and I slipped into the bathroom, and I closed the door behind us. I flipped on the fan and turned to face her in that tiny room. She smelled like cotton candy, and I chained my arms at my side so as not to scoop her up and pull her close right then.

As our eyes met, she blushed.

"You wanna' go first," she offered, holding the sploof and Batsy's pipe up as she did.

"I need to see you do it," I replied. "I'm not sure I'm clear on how to use the sploof."

"Oh, yeah. Sure," she said. It was quite simple. "Take a hit, then pick up the sploof and exhale through it." While watching her make it, I thought the pipe was supposed to be sheathed inside the cardboard tube.

We laughed at my expense as I explained this.

Her laugh… I can barely hear it anymore. I recall a fragment of its auditory bliss, but I can still see it… and in that moment, under the shadow of her cap, her sapphire stars lit up my world as I lit up the pipe.

The clouds we exhaled billowed up to the ventilation fan in a tumble, like Charlie and Grandpa in Wonka's Fizzy Lifting Room. The clouds in our lungs went straight to our heads.

"You have a really clean bathroom," she admired. I process a lot of my anxiety by cleaning: a habit inherited from my mother's family. At the time, I had no idea; I just thought others were not keeping up on the cleaning.

A big, dumb grin spread across my face in a pathetic pooling of muscles. "I like a clean place – I've seen some real shitty living situations in this town… especially from other men.

Saidey shivered with disgust. "Seriously, though," was all she added.

Our eyes connected. At the same time, we both inhaled sharply. Saidey smiled sweetly. If her eyelids hadn't been heavy with THC, she may have batted them. There was my opening.

Kiss her, you *fucking* coward, my brain shouted from the cheap seats. I settled my groundlings.

I'd waited over a week to get back to a moment like this, and her energy seemed to invite the time alone, even if she wouldn't make the first move. I knew I was expected to, but the thought of being stopped or pushed back made my nerves lurch; a mole burrowed into my stomach.

My insides danced.

Tell her how you feel, I thought. "Hey," I stammered slightly, "I just–"

Someone knocked on the bathroom door. We both jumped, and I nearly dropped the pipe.

"Jerry? Big Jay is here." It was dear Edwyn.

I swung the door wide. Edwyn was standing off to the right, and the rest of the doorway was empty. But Big Jay was hard to miss. He was a distinct gent, and he towered over us.

"Well, hello," his voice said mischievously.

Quickly, my eyes darted down to the source.

Big Jay's head was at ground level.

The stairs up to the second floor traced an exterior wall but then hooked a right angle, ending up in the middle of the upstairs hallway. The bathroom was a quick righthand U-turn around the corner at the top of the stairwell. Big Jay had stopped on the landing halfway up the steps to lie himself stomach down so that only his head appeared to us in the corner of the doorway. He was just a human head on the floor with good hair and a strong profile, accented by the charming crook in his nose.

"Oh, my God," Saidey proclaimed, pointing in surprise. We all burst out laughing, but I caught Saidey's cheeks flash petunia pink. Butterflies tickled my heart. She was embarrassed, too, which meant she thought something was about to happen.

Dammit!

"Whatcha' doing in there," Big Jay asked. His tone was curious – the type of curious that resonates in a voice when a parent has caught a child playing with something dangerous. He was being playful, but I felt his energy. He had a skeptical eyebrow raised at me, like Icarus's wingman fretting over the heat on his pilot's waxen instruments.

"Just a little *Prometheus* pre-gaming," I said quickly with a casual air. "Didn't wanna' stink the place up for the roommates," I added, holding up the sploof.

"Nice," Big Jay nodded, satisfied with that explanation as he pushed himself up to his feet. "May I," he asked.

"Yeah, dude, get in here."

Edwyn excused himself. Green wasn't his scene.

"You know how to use one of these," Saidey asked, holding up the sploof.

"Exhale through the tube, right?"

"Yep." She handed it to him, and we stepped out so he could sneak in. Saidey glanced at me bashfully while the door was closed, but I knew we didn't have time to act.

Was I daydreaming, or did her expression seem to confess

that she was disappointed we'd been interrupted?

Could I see a thing like that in someone's eyes?

That was the end of our alone time, apart from snickers and snark shared between us. Our faces drew nearer and nearer to divulge each joke while Ridley Scott danced around his not-prequel concept for the first hour of screen time. During the film's climax, actor Noomi Rapace had to run away from a crashing horseshoe-shaped spaceship as it rolled forward on its rounded hull.

The shot had the actress running directly at camera, in a straight path underneath the rolling craft. It was painfully clear in that moment that, if the character Elizabeth Shaw just took a sharp left or right turn, she'd avoid the path of the tumbling craft altogether. Instead, she melodramatically outruns the massive object through some unexplained feat of physics. Simultaneously, Saidey and I scoffed a subtle but critical, "What?"

We caught each other's eyes and laughed, leaning in for another whisper. "She could have just run to the side!"

"Either side!"

Our faces were closer than ever. We were expressing our disbelief at the spaceship spectacle, but the way she held my gaze, the intimate proximity of her smile… and her crystalline eyes…were intoxicating. I was not imagining things, I thought. The tension of desire magnetized between us. Jay seemed focused on the movie, maybe he wouldn't notice if we had a moment.

Nope. I felt a side-eye swing our way. It wasn't accusatory, just Big Jay distracted by my movement, but it immediately erased any illusion of privacy. Saidey broke eye contact with me as she saw him, shaking her head about the spaceship, and that was the end of our moment. There would be no more chances in that screening. Regardless, it was a damn good time. I spent the first third of the movie so stoned, I experienced a weird tunnel vision that made the theater melt away. There was the film, and there was my seat and there was Saidey to my right. The rest bled into the shadows of Plato's Cave, and I sat back to watch my youth flicker by. Perhaps that's why the rolling spaceship is the most distinct memory I have of the screening. But I suspect it was the moment with Saidey that burned the memory into my skull.

Big Jay dropped us off at my place and headed home, but only after we all talked about the movie a little bit. She was fun to watch movies with. She even had a willing suspension of disbelief very attuned to my own. She was sharp, and she was fun and intelligent and stimulating. After fun spent talking about the movie during our shop hours on Friday, my heart and stomach took turns doing flips all weekend as I waited to see her again on Monday.

Self-criticism was also heavy on my heart. Edwyn had been the only person I had divulged my secret crush to, and he was back home, so I didn't have a chance to talk to him in person. He'd only met Saidey briefly, in May for Shy's night and for the shop movie night. Beyond that, he'd only crossed paths with us. I called him to talk about it – his reactions were gentle, but in line with what my conscience was doing. While he seemed to consider Kelly Joe a friend, he also knew the frustrations I faced in that partnership. Regardless, we pondered the morality of my urges, concluding that I didn't want to be like that.

There was already a terrible trope in society that said, "It's not a matter of *if* a man will cheat, but a matter of *when*." I grew up watching my uncles ruin relationships and family dynamics with their flippant cock-pleasing, and I disdained them for it from the age of nine. What's more, the high school sweetheart I lost my virginity to went emotionally AWOL just three months shy of our two-year anniversary, running around after work with other guys from other high schools and growing distant with me, the person who had helped her through two suicide attempts. I had to break things off because she wouldn't answer me when I'd ask what was wrong. The distance she put between us was cold and painful, yet still she went through the motions.

She had shared her email password with me, and when I realized she was lying to me, I logged in and poked around. A word of advice: if you're the cheating type, don't give your partner your passwords. I have undone the lies of two committed relationships by simply logging in and poking around for the truth.

I had felt like absolute dirt – no, worse. I felt like the bedrock underneath dirt when I found those suggestive messages. What I know now, though, is that most people act that way when they subconsciously want out of a relationship. They can't be honest with themselves or confront the truth, so they close themselves off from their partner instead. It's easier to keep moving forward if you don't turn to face the damage in your wake. Hurting Kelly Joe felt wrong, especially while she was working to build a musician's resume and pad our savings a little more for the big move to New York.

I also had no idea at the time, but I have, throughout life, put other people's needs and wants before my own. A peace-keeper, a diplomacy-wielder. I would make myself or my own needs smaller to accommodate the concerns of anyone else.

What I wanted was to amplify the connection with Saidey. She was exciting – edgy – and there was something about the crackle between us. I couldn't recall that kind of 'live wire' when Kelly Joe and I had started seeing each other. She'd broken it off with me twice in the first six weeks together. Twice, I'd pursued, spilling my guts to her on several occasions. It was, in part, my own young hunt for validation that I suspect drove me to pursue Kelly Joe like I did. I should have just let go. Two chances within six weeks I had. I could have just let her walk out of my life before she could do any damage. I should have just moved on.

Ah, but if I had, reason pervaded, I wouldn't have had a

reason to stay in Black Swamp longer, and I likely would not have pursued grad school… meaning that, without Kelly Joe in the picture, I would have never even met Saidey. My heart sank further. There was no, 'if only.' Saidey and I had been doomed to our star-crossed path in this one and only butterfly effect. Had I not chased Kelly Joe and built a serious relationship, I would not have decided to live in Black Swamp to wait out her graduation. If none of that had happened, I would not have had the bright idea to pursue graduate school while I had the resources and the time to do it. Without grad school, there'd have been no theater cross-over, no scene shop work, and no Saidey. I'd have left Black Swamp two years prior.

I sighed. The problem was exhausting from every angle. I had not the character to cheat. I am not built that way. If she initiated, which I suspected by now was not her way of operating, then I knew I would not fight it. But I couldn't for the life of me make myself kiss another woman, no matter how natural it felt in every fiber of my very being. My spirit wailed, bemoaning the whole damnable mess. It was all my fault, too. I had pursued her – I had found reasons to interact over and over… hell, even when we were discussing the props for the film, I knew it was an excuse to be associated with her. That film never materialized, scrapped for practicality's sake, but it had been the bonding agent I needed to become better friends with her.

My heart ached thinking about all the laughs and smiles shared between us. I wanted to know what it felt like to be her boyfriend. I was deathly afraid she'd find some hip, too-cool-for-school artist dude who knew he was hot shit, and I'd be toast in a matter of months because I knew I was worthless and found the human ego to be a hollow, impish prig.

I wanted to be with Saidey. I admitted it to myself head-on. I was willing to make myself uncomfortable over and over again to try and get that romantic fuse to hiss and crackle all the way to the dynamite I was planting under my wedding. Did I really have it in me to tank a whole wedding? I'd spent so much on the rings – so much was booked and ready for late August. Friends had already booked flights, Big Jay included.

Edwyn wasn't sure what else to offer me. He couldn't tell if she liked me, though he agreed the signs suggested it, and wasn't sure it mattered. He thought perhaps I was getting cold feet about the wedding, which he reassured me was perfectly natural, from what we'd heard. In the end, he sighed heavily with sorrow; he couldn't offer much advice. "I know you, though," he reassured, "and you'll do what's right."

My cynical, self-loathing side rolled his eyes. Such a cranky fellow. But cynical Jerry was defending my own desires. I didn't want to do what was right.

I wanted to seize the day.

To seize my youth.

To kiss Saidey.

You've already admitted your urge to be with her, my stormy mind continued reasoning with itself. There was no turning back from that. Perhaps that's why I had told Edwyn; I needed to hear it out loud and confront the truth. Plus, my optimistic side chipped in, there's no way we spend all summer in town together without another chance to kiss.

That was all I really wanted. I wanted to kiss her and feel her kiss back: to know that she welcomed it – that she wanted it, too. That's all my heart needed, truly. Anything more intimate was improbable, spectacular, and part of my wildest dreams only. That would have meant a boost like no other for my sad ego (that impish prig!).

The silly ways we measure things…

Kelly Joe had continually made me uncomfortable with her philosophies on performed intimacy, insisting that there were many things we should both be okay with. I never had an option, you understand.

She simply told me how things were going to be.

Since I was a damned fool, I listened – surrendered all agency to keep her happy. Was a kiss – or even kissing – truly harmful in the grand scheme of things if I intended to be with Kelly Joe for the rest of my waking hours?

Yes, wisdom told me. A stage kiss should not carry emotion, whereas there was no way for my person to kiss Saidey in that way. Not with my tangled emotions.

Back and forth my mind went, a thought and a half per second, unrelenting in its torment of my heart.

☙ ❧

Putting my memories back together in order has been tricky. I saved very little to document that summer and have spent countless hours digging up old notes and calendars to piece things together. I don't even have a picture with her. If there was more between us over the course of the next week, I truly can't recall.

Suffice it to say, schoolwork, fiancé, and scene shop hours kept me juggling my commitments. Then, on Wednesday morning, we were dancing in each other's orbits until the morning fifteen. Or perhaps I was the satellite twirling through her vibrant pink magnetic field. Either way.

The morning fifteen was just a cigarette break. Danny was a heavy smoker and he had worked as a stage technician in the local unions out of Cincinnati prior to getting hired at Black Swamp. As a result, he had built union-standard smoke breaks into the shop schedule at two-hour intervals. The crew was in at seven, and on the loading dock by nine for that first break.

During those moments, I would hang with Danny. I didn't mind the second-hand smoke, even enjoyed it a little when it mixed with the smell of my coffee and the lingering freshness of grass clippings. What's more, he had excellent stories, and he had taken a liking to sharing most all of them with me. We were buds more than he was my boss, and he wasn't worried about respect; he knew I respected the shit out of him. Anyway, I was also relishing in those smoke breaks – those tidbits of my day when the wiser, more interesting man I looked up to would open up his mental Cabinet of Curiosities and pluck some wild story from its shelves for me.

Before I made it to my post, Saidey intercepted. "You and Big Jay seeing any movies this week?"

I shrugged, but I was flailing inside like Kermit the Frog doing his happy flaps. "Nothing new out," I reported. "We already saw the Wes Anderson film when it came out, and we don't have anything else on our list that's out yet."

"What are your feelings on that Snow White movie that just came out?"

I wrinkled up my nose, cautious not to trash something the lady liked. There's nothing quite as demoralizing as having someone you liked tear one of your interests to shreds… Kelly Joe had taught me that firsthand. "It did pique my interest," I admitted, which was true. "I love the dark retelling of fairy tales, particularly if it comes from the Grimms, since those were all so damn dark to begin with." She smiled at me as I explained. "But I don't want to give it any money because I can't stand Kristen Stewart's performances."

"Oh, God, me too! I, uh… I kinda' wanted to see it *because* it's a trainwreck. That's the kind of movie to really get stoned for," she added with a grin.

"Well, when you put it *that* way, I'm definitely interested," I flirted. My heart wanted to burst into a musical number. Another movie outing, and she had initiated it. That was good, right?

Yes, of course it's bloody-well good! What's bloody-well awful is that you haven't made a move yet, my cynical pathos barked back.

"Big Jay's invited, too," she added reassuringly. That killed the wind in my sails, and my mind went flogging about in Saidey's shifting gales.

"That might not be his thing, but you should ask him at

lunch," I encouraged. "Besides, I'm in either way *but* I have one condition."

"Oh, you have conditions now?" She smirked, an unadulterated flirtation, and the hammer in my heart thrummed like war drums. "Shoot," she challenged.

"I need free reign to riff hard on the expressionless, vapid void that is Kristen Stewart's 'acting face.' If that's cool, I will definitely take you to see that."

Whoa. My thoughts shuddered to a screeching halt. I'd spent so much time in my head imagining a relationship with her, I was slipping in the real world. The wording of that was bold – it could be enough to weird her out.

"Deal!" With that, she shook on it, then crossed out of the shop, most likely making for the restrooms before break ended. I don't recall any other details until the following night because I was urging time to scream by at the speed of sound...

9. RECKLESS ABANDON

Next with Jay we slipped away
To see Snow White in our own way.
She was there first so we might smoke,
Used dryer sheets for bathroom tokes.
We laughed so hard we nearly cried
When in a milk bath Theron lied.
Stewart stared on, unaffected,
While we jeered and interjected.
Such fun we had; was it just me?
Had I inhaled far too much weed?
Or was this girl my destiny?
A bond of potent chemistry
Like I had not yet known in youth.
If only she would steal my truth.
Alas, we were not left alone
To explore our great unknowns.
Her eyes, they blazed all steely blue
Telling me, "I'd be with you."
If only I had grabbed the hint,
Given those eyes reason to glint.

Instead, I let the credits roll,
And so, regret torments my soul…

After the credits, Saidey marveled at Kristen Stewart's hollow performance. "I've never really watched her and paid attention to what bugs me, but you're right; she just kind of stares off blankly and it's supposed to mean something."

I simply smiled. Saidey got it.

Big Jay and Saidey joined me at Wayne Manor after the movie. We agreed we were all hungry, so we ordered from Pisanello's, our favorite local pizza joint. We got stoned as we waited, chilling in the living room with one dim lamp on in the corner.

I packed our glass pipe and handed it to Big Jay, who took a puff, then passed it to me. I took a hit and shared some observation about the movie that I can't now recall.

"Hey," Saidey said firmly, "remember, it's a pipe, not a talking stick." She gestured for me to pass the piece.

"Right, sorry." I said.

Big Jay laughed, waited until I took my hit and passed the pipe, then said, "What are the numbers, Jerry?"

"Oh, man. Don't," I pleaded.

"C'mon, just… just tell us the numbers."

"I don't want to."

"What is this," Saidey said, giggling. "Is this some trick you do or something?"

"Jerry, what are the numbers," Big Jay encouraged again.

Saidey's expectant smirk convinced me to cave in.

"Four, eight, fifteen, sixteen, twenty-three, forty-two."

Saidey's giggles boiled over. "What?"

"One more time for our guest, Jerry?" Big Jay had that mischief in his eye now.

"Four, eight, fifteen, sixteen, twenty-three, forty-two," I repeated. He accepted the pipe from Saidey and took his second hit.

"Why are you doing that," Saidey asked.

"Because he tricked me," I proclaimed. "He tricked me into learning those damn numbers."

"You were obsessing with the numbers on the microwave clock," he divulged, nodding to the microwave behind her, where the counter ended, and the living room began. We had the couch dividing it from the open kitchen behind.

"I was time-traveling," I shot back. "*That* was fun," I teased.

Saidey guffawed. "What are the numbers from? Why do I know that?"

"They're the fucking numbers from *Lost*. The Valenzetti numbers that show up all over the show – the same ones that are supposed to mathematically predict the end of the world," I said, annoyed that I knew that much about the stinking combination.

Big Jay snickered, pleased with himself.

Saidey toppled over laughing as I tried to pass the pipe back to her. "You guys are too much," she struggled through her amusement. I grinned at her glee as I held the pipe, waiting for her to recover from her laughing fits and sit upright again.

The doorbell rang and I stiffened up to perform 'sobriety' for the pizza delivery guy. Saidey popped up behind me, putting her hands out to touch my back. Not in a playful way, just so I knew she was there.

"I can take those," she offered as the teenager unloaded the two pizzas from his tattered red carrier.

He was young, pimply and thin. But he was chill. He sniffed the air as it wafted out from the apartment, then took closer note of Saidey. From there, I felt him watching me enviously as I signed the receipt and gave him a generous tip.

That satisfied grin hooked my left cheek as I handed him his copy. "Have an excellent night, dude," I said with a smile. Wow, I thought as I cradled our two-liter of soda, I'm so high, I'm on top of the world; even the pizza guy was jealous of me.

I could feel it. How did I get here? How long could I sustain such a thing? Was that what all this was? I'd been in town for six years, and I'd mastered quite a few quirks of living cheap and sucking all the marrow possible from Black Swamp's higher education system.

Eventually, I'd have to move on. Eventually, it wouldn't be cool, it would be weird… maybe even creepy… and Saidey wouldn't make me stay *that* long. One more year was nothing. Maybe Danny would hire me as shop staff since I was already on-track to graduate the English master's program in mid-August.

My heart ached, mulling over my future as we sat and talked and ate our food, the three of us. Somewhere in there, we all fell asleep. When I woke up on the floor, Big Jay had just risen out of the plush armchair he'd occupied since dinner. The whole living room was dark. Jay was heading down the hallway for the front door.

"See you at lunch," he asked in a whisper.

"You know it," I whispered back, and he slipped out, locking the doorknob behind him for me. I was on the floor at the foot of the couch, where Saidey had curled up.

The click of the door woke up Saidey, and she pushed herself up on the couch, smiling at me in the darkness as I stood.

It was four-thirty.

"Did he *just* leave," she asked, nodding at Big Jay's empty chair.

"Yep."

"But, why now? The night's more than half over."

I shrugged. "He lives right across Main Street. He prefers his own bed. Never really crashes somewhere all night."

"Well, I hope it's okay if I stay right here."

"Unless you'd prefer the futon downstairs for more room," I offered. Edwyn was stuck back at his parents' home again.

"No, thanks," she said, tossing onto her side, "this is a great couch." It was a great couch.

"If you're up first, don't hesitate to wake me, okay?"

"Got it. Will do," she said as she rolled over.

I smiled, slipping into the restroom on the first floor. When I came back out, she was already asleep again. It had grown chilly overnight, so I retrieved my Turtles sleeping bag from the corner and covered her with it. Then, I ascended to my own chambers.

I left my bedroom door open. I wanted to feel accessible to my guest if she needed anything. My friends were gentlemen, but she was still a young lady asleep in a townhouse full of boys. It was important that she felt safe.

ଓ ଛ

Later that morning, I was the first one up. For a moment, I lie there daydreaming that she would come up and confess our mutual feelings and seize the morning together. Instead, I heard an unfamiliar but gentle snore echo up to me through the lofted hallway from our living room.

Sunrise blazed a faint citrus orange glow outside, catching dust that hadn't settled from its nighttime dance across the loft.

Groggily, I approached the top of the stairs. Shop hours had shifted to eight since we were no longer racing the heat of the day in those old buildings at U-hall. If I got coffee started, she'd be up within thirty minutes and we could spend the morning together, I reasoned.

So, delicate as a cat in the night, I unpacked my coffee provisions from my cupboard over the sink and loaded my little orange drip machine. It made enough for three mugs of coffee: more than enough for us both. Easing the cupboards closed again, I flipped on the power for my coffeemaker. After a few hearty hisses and a splutter, the drip machine helped Saidey slowly come-to. She saw me as she sat up, stretching her arms over her shoulders.

"Morning," she said quietly. Was she just the slightest bit more girly in her sleepy state, or was I merely drunk with adoration?

"Hey," is all my dumb ass spluttered back. "Coffee'll be ready soon," I reassured, trying to recover from that.

"You rock," she said softly. Then, her sleep-filled gaze fell on the chair where Big Jay had been sleeping. "Oh, yeah," she said pointing. "He left at like four in the morning, didn't he?" She was pointing at Big Jay's empty seat.

"Yeah," I nodded sharply.

She squinted at the clock. "Why?" She must not have been fully awake when I told her earlier.

I shrugged. "Big Jay doesn't like to spend a whole overnight somewhere else. Plus, his place it just a seven-minute walk straight across North Main." I was careful to whisper, so as not to wake my roommates.

She nodded, considering this reasonable enough.

We sat and had coffee quietly, a few knowing glances and bashful smiles shared over steaming mugs. She didn't leave until it was time for us to get to work. So, from six fifteen to seven forty, we nursed our mugs and, I suspect now, nursed our very mutual crush.

I offered the showers so she could just go straight to work with me, but she wanted her own fresh clothes for the summer heat. We left my place together, and she lingered while I locked up, hugging me goodbye before we drove to work separately, only to reconvene in the shop.

I was right on time… she was five minutes late. When she saw me, she smiled wide, looking straight into my eyes as she walked in. "That coffee was great," she whispered to me as she passed. "I feel wide awake!"

For whatever reason, I cannot recall why we never saw each other on weekends. I know I spent Saturdays up in Sandusky keeping Kelly Joe happy. Perhaps Saidey was taking trips home to see her mom? Or maybe she liked to hang with her roommate. I don't honestly know. Time has blurred such details.

All I know is I usually didn't hear from Saidey on weekends, not even then, which is why I was surprised to get a text from her that Sunday night, June 18th. I was home… upstairs scribbling another story. Perhaps this was "I'm bored: Take 2," I told myself. Please let it be that.

'Can I call u quick?' It was maybe a quarter after nine. We had all night to talk or meet up or… maybe finally…

'Of course. U don't have to ask. Haha,' I replied immediately.

The phone rang in seconds.

"Hey," I answered, "what's on your mind?" Could it be that she was calling to confront our truth? To confess her crush or ask about mine? The monkey in my chest clenched at my throat, squeezing it shut.

Here comes the storm, Alice reached out to tell me.

I won't lie, I promised myself. I'll tell her the truth about how I feel. I can't run from this. She's too great.

"I wanted your input on something," she divulged.

"Okay, sure. Yeah. Shoot," I encouraged.

"I got a job offer, but if I take it, I'd only be able to give Danny one week's notice. This upcoming week would have to be my last in the shop."

"Congrats, that's so cool," I uttered, trying not to feel sick *and* dizzy with disappointment. I was choking in my head. "What – uh – what's the gig?"

"It's an art summer camp out in Vermont." she was so excited. I wanted to shriek when I felt the sadness sink its claws into my pectorals and drag them through me like black pearl daggers through my soul.

"That's so great." *Fucking liar.*

"Yeah," she cheered, "and I *have* to take it."

I wanted to cry. "I think Danny will understand

completely. This is how college art gigs go. My only suggestion would be to write him a formal email tonight, and then go see him to follow up about it first-thing tomorrow morning. That way, he'll know you sincerely gave him as much notice as you possibly could. He'll be cool."

"Yeah, you're right. Thank you!"

A band of creeping creatures paraded through my broken heart, rinsing sadness through all my limbs as reality set in. I was doomed – I was already committed to go up to Cedar Point again on Saturday, even though I would have rather stayed in my crow's nest there atop Unit D1 at Wayne Manor.

"And," Saidey added, "I'm still around until next Wednesday. I mean, I have to pack starting Saturday because now I'm moving out of this apartment early, but–

"Friday," I said. "My place. Let's have one more Halo night. Movies, weed, cotton candy, you name it."

"That sounds amazing," she said. I could hear her excitement was genuine, but I wasn't sure exactly where it originated.

"I'll see you in the morning," I said with as much sincerity as my frozen heart could muster.

Just like that, my chances to be with her were cut down to one final week of work and one glorious final hangout on Friday, June 22nd, 2012.

Saidey showed up early, just like she had for Shy's night. She wasn't able to hang any weeknight prior because her prepping and packing and moving was more than she'd anticipated. I wasn't sure I should offer to help or not. Maybe I did, but she was sorting everything out on her own.

We hiked the suburban sprawl over to Kroger. It was just across two parking lots and North Main. There, we collected the staples to a fun night: cotton candy tubs, chips and dip, and cheese puffs. When we got back, it was still just the two of us, so we smoked down in the basement in order to hang the 'Don't Come In: I'm GAMING' door-knob hanger one more time… one more round of Halo.

I ordered the pizzas and got lost in her eyes a little longer before Batsford came home from a rehearsal. He hopped right into our smoking circle. Big Jay filtered in next, rubbing his hands together in anticipation of our very own five-cheese pizza invention.

Once everyone had gathered, we kept the party to the living room with the sliding door wide and the fresh night air rolling in to purify our altered minds. The pizzas arrived and we feasted. Somewhere in there, Saidey realized she hadn't noticed my fiddler crabs before.

"How did I miss that?" And I was following her up to my room. This was my chance. Alone in my room long enough to tell her the truth. After five seconds, though, Batsford came up to join us. He was in the musical theater program with Kelly Joe – how could I signal to him to get lost? That was far too crass an action to take. I willed him to buzz off telepathically, but he seemed unreceptive. I blamed the weed and grumbled to myself.

After that, I cut loose. I had another hit so long I nearly cached the bowl with my first and only draw. We had a few beers, not much because I didn't want the night's memories to be too fuzzy. It was enough, though. Enough to get me angry at the world.

I excused myself out the back door and pissed all over the patio of our neighbors who shared the back lawn with us. Their kids had put a baseball through my windshield back in April and no one had the nerve to tell me, so I had to pay for it on my own instead. Fuck that.

I didn't let anyone come with, but I told them what I'd done when I returned. They laughed in disbelief. Then, I decided I should shave my growing beard into a different style of facial hair. Saidey suggested I should do it in phases.

Anything to amuse you, my dear.

First, I shaved only my chin, so my moustache was

attached to weak mutton chop sideburns. I came out to reveal it, then did a Macho Man Randy Savage impression because it felt right. Everyone voted next for me to 'shave the chops but keep the long sideburns.'

"And keep the moustache!" Saidey clarified.

The room laughed in agreement.

The result? I appeared, to them, like a seventy's porn star. I found the cheap orange Aviator sunglasses I still had from my performance as Hunter S. Thompson three years prior, reappearing at the top of the stairs for everyone. The persona was complete with the pursing of my lips at everyone. The room recoiled, laughing all the while. They were like putty in my hands. How I loved to perform like that – to bring joy like some magic spell over a parlor of like-minded intelligence. I glowed.

Saidey howled, crying, and laughing and wiping her eyes through the night. At one point, not sure if she was crying or laughing, I asked if she was okay.

"Yeah," she smirked. "I haven't laughed this hard in a while," she observed, wiping the sides of her face. "I am definitely gonna' miss this," she added through chuckles. She wiped her eyes again. If there was more to it than that, I missed it completely.

Retreating into the bathroom, I shaved down to my desired length of sideburns and cleaned up to just a bushy moustache. Spurred on by Saidey's joy – her beat-red, tear-streaked face – I embraced my goofiness. Lying on the floor on my side and facing my friends, I worked my upper lip up the side of our coffee table leg so my moustache would appear to them as a fuzzy caterpillar climbing to our food scraps.

Batsford took a video, which he shared with me years later. I recall I was struck by the howling laughter coming from Saidey. She was hysterical, and at one moment, I was struck by how she looked at me then. Somehow, I hadn't let myself see all of it in the moment. Hell, at that time in the night, all I really remember seeing is the leg of the coffee table.

Batsford retreated to his room first, then Big Jay sauntered home. We sat together for just a little longer, finishing our beers. That was dragged out another twenty minutes as we talked. Reluctance hung heavy in the air until finally Saidey admitted she was tired, too. I was disappointed, thinking it early, but it was just after one in the morning.

I walked her out to her car, fighting again with myself to confess my truth to her.

Kiss her goodbye, I thought. There's still a chance during your goodbye… but I stayed the dutiful, committed coward. I told her I'd miss her, she promised we'd keep in touch, and we held each other close in a rigid but desperate hug to save the moment.

As we separated, I peered deep in her eyes.

"If you ever want to visit New York," was all I managed.

She smiled. "I will," she said.

The spark from our night in the theater was nowhere in sight in that empty parking lot. At least, that's what I convinced myself. That's why I let the moment pass.

After she drove away, I put my music in my headphones, and my feet roved all over that parking lot thinking about her. If ghosts are just a compressing of atomic memory from repeated habits, there is still a haunted young man roaming the parking lot of the Hillsdale Apartments.

Denying that romance with her felt like the death of my youth. I did the thing she hated; I made the adult decision. Not to say that such fortitude is austere, but in this specific case, I believe the opposite choice could have saved me.

Her eyes. They were so crystal clear. Brilliant blue. And for three months, I'd stolen time swimming in them, dragged out into their mighty riptide. I wanted to share whatever pain I sensed behind them; to make it go away, chased off by that best medicine, laughter.

When would I see those eyes again?

Would I ever?

My heart squawked sadly as it leapt out of my throat and flapped in death throes on the late-night lawn. The moon frowned for us as I watched my shriveled blood-muscle quiver, fighting for air. In such scenarios, it is best not to intervene, and so I watched my little heart-beast wither and die under the night's deathly pale lunar glow.

೧ ೨

One night that July, after going up to Huron Playhouse to see a show, I landed at the *Miami Biker Bar* on some empty backroad in a boggy field to catch up with Shy. All that night, I was with Danny and Shy again – hanging out and bullshitting together one last time before I shuffled off into the wide world. But being around them only made me think of her.

At that point, she'd been gone for a month, and my time at school was drawing to a close. I stirred up Saidey's name with Shy, only to find that she was no longer of interest to him.

"I just think I dropped the ball there way too much," he said. "She's great, but…" he shrugged, then took a sip of his beer. "…I missed the boat. It's totally my fault. I think that ship sailed before the spring semester ended. She kinda stopped texting back in March."

You don't say, Shy. You don't say.

My heart swelled and ached all at once. I suspected that poor Shy's unanswered texts coincided with Saidey's interest in me. Hearing it confirmed was like a kick in the balls. She had absolutely had a crush on me. Maybe not an exclusive one, but it had been enough to redirect her attention.

She had been right there with me for months. Now, she was somewhere out in Vermont – at a summer camp in the middle of nowhere… with a bunch of hip artist dudes. She was her own person. But it hurt to think about.

I'd been right there alongside her all night… multiple

times… up late… alone. I mean, fuck, the girl had crashed with me more than once. Was I really that dense, or had I been too nervous of the consequences?

My heart flip-flopped again. I wanted to jump in my car and drive until I found her. Instead, I sat with my friend and had another drink, and life forged ahead.

10. DOGS EATING DOGS

June 2013.

Saidey and I kept in loose contact via text, sending maybe three updates to each other over the course of that year. She'd just graduated that spring and was working locally – staying connected to projects and teachers at Black Swamp's College of Fine Arts. At one point, she admitted that my own ingenuity inspired her decision to save for a move to a big city by working close to her academic resources.

I was sitting at my desk in the corner of my living room – a pleasantly-sized one-bedroom apartment in Inwood[9] – it even had a foyer with extra closets. My writing desk was nestled in a nook created by the interior corner of the living room, the quietest possible spot in the whole place.

Unemployed, I was surfing the job postings on Playbill, hoping to capitalize on all my recent Broadway management credentials when my phone started ringing. To my surprise, it was Saidey. So far as I knew, she never called anyone on the phone. Completely avoided social media, too… and, as I had

---

[9] The northernmost neighborhood in modern Manhattan.

learned over the last year, she didn't seem to check her emails very often, either.

There is not much that needs recounted with regards to my now-ex-wife, Kelly Joe, and how we spent July 2012 through June 2013. In short, she and I wrapped up at Black Swamp, got married in September of 2012 and kicked off our marriage by arguing about the lack of sex on our honeymoon and the lack of money in our bank accounts… two pain-points that would ring true throughout our plague-riddled matrimony.

We moved to New York City in a torrential downpour – a mood that permeated our time there together – crashed on couches for weeks until we locked in an apartment – the aforementioned Inwood crib. I was unemployed for the first three months, excepting a few short freelance gigs. Kelly Joe made monetary contributions to the household by begrudgingly teaching music to spoiled upper-class toddlers. I could never blame her for disliking that gig – the parents were demanding and extremely entitled, and it extended to the personalities of their three-year-olds. But what she hated was any gig involving her instrument. She wanted to perform – to act, and dance and sing. Very few people were interested beyond her niche folk skills, to the point where she stopped accepting gigs involving her mandolin. Just as she was making more money for it, too.

So, we ate through savings. My savings. The nest-egg I managed to put together for us during graduate school – bolstered by generous support from our wedding gifts, of course – was devoured within six months of getting by. Voice lessons twice a month or more – that was hundreds of dollars – and then new headshots, new resume print-offs because we couldn't afford a printer, rehearsal room rentals for shooting audition reels, rehearsal room rentals for rehearsing audition pieces; on and on the list of Kelly's necessary expenses grew.

Our rent was $1300 a month, plus the fees of internet and utilities. That probably sounds like a dream now, ten years later, but I assure you it was very high for two struggling artists with no reliable full-time income or health insurance. We weren't in a great area, but that didn't become apparent until eight months in, when the days warmed up and everyone seemed to go wild. There were gang fights on the fire escape outside our bedroom windows, gunplay over the meth cooking one floor down, and, perhaps more aggravating than all of it, the constant block parties in the little pedestrian alley between our buildings. These parties would start around 11 a.m. on one day and go until 3 a.m. or 5 a.m. the next. Thursdays through Sundays in warm weather, it would thunder soundwaves of tinny Latino pop music at us. The bassline chord progression was identical nearly every song. It nearly drove me to insanity on several occasions. Once, I even put my computer speakers out the window and pumped *It's a Small World* into the alley. It was so unsettling that I ended my attack after only five excruciating minutes of auditory Hell.

At the beginning of May 2013, I'd narrowly escaped a mugging by two imposing but dull-headed teenagers on my way to work. Filing the police report for that with NYPD was such a pain in the ass, I vowed to just punch my assailant and run if it happened again.

Admittedly, I was feeling lost. I couldn't get work as an actor or as a writer, and the people I witnessed doing that hustle were not as skilled or polished as I felt I was. Many of them were more musical, though. Music has always been the muse who vexes most, and not for my lack of trying. It was even the inadequacy Kelly Joe later cited as 'the thing she couldn't get over.' Yes, of all the arts, music eluded me – taunting me from afar like a girl afraid to admit she had a crush.

Perhaps that's why being in the industry of the American musical was so gratifying, albeit subconsciously then. Thanks to a hard-working, socially voracious friend Jeffrey Spalding, I booked a paid internship at Made2Measure Theatricals. As a result, the first four and a half months of 2013 had been sheer showbiz bliss: my career was ahead of me and shaping up to be quite glamorous. I racked up Playbill credits for the Motown Musical (met Barry Gordy and half of Motown's living legends), *Breakfast at Tiffany's* (met Emelia Clark during rehearsals), *Let It Be* (a Beatles tribute), and Barry Manilow's one-man show. Even *Mamma Mia*! *The* Mamma Mia – the same one that opened in 2001 and had over five thousand seven hundred performances[10].

The back of my head even popped up in photos at Manilow's opening night because I worked the front door outside the Copa Cabana – where the dazzling opening night party was held (obviously). But the reality of show blight set in fast once I jumped in with three days to train and replace a tenacious office manager and producer's assistant named Jason, who had been with the rotten scrooge Maximos Klauditius[11] for seven years. Jason was a cunning young man with self-proclaimed 'expensive taste' who saw all the money in advertising on Broadway. He'd pried a position at Plotco[12] from someone else's hands thanks to a personal connection through an ex-lover. I only know this because he bragged about it while he was training me. I told everyone at that company I was a scribe; I cannot help it that they felt inclined to indulge their secrets anyway.

"They say the lights are bright on Broadway…"

Anyway, Jason was out and the 'nice boy from the Ohio school' was in. Maxi had a boner for the fact that I went to Black Swamp University… his parents immigrated from

---

[10] It finally closed in 2015, two years after being moved out of the mighty Winter Garden Theater and into the Broadhurst.

[11] If it sounds like a venereal disease when you pronounce it in your head, you're pronouncing it right. And he was a disease, the miserable, cheap, cheating bastard.

[12] *The* go-to Broadway advertising firm. Producers budget for it so their show seems posh. Otherwise, they look cheap. Maxi used Plotco begrudgingly for this very reason. "It's all on the computer these days. Can't we just hire a college kid?"

Greece to the United States right after he was born, worked until they could buy a small farm in western Ohio, and raised him there. He hadn't been home in decades, and he was so fixated on my education at a proud Ohio school, that he glazed over the Pittsburgh upbringing. It was all 'hard-working country,' that's all Maxi cared about.

I had been hired as the full-time office manager of his boutique Broadway producer's office and stand-by Assistant Production Manager for several self-contained Broadway shows. There was the limited-run revival of Billy Crystal's one-man show, *700 Weekends* and the somewhat successful *Jukebox Billie.* The nasty old Greek bigot who owned Nikolas Companies, was so cheap, he had the script reworked to reappropriate the Billie Holiday story when the singer's successors refused to license their grandmother's likeness. So, Maxi and the writer wrote the character as Billie Holidae. Apparently it was much cheaper to license the rights to perform the artist's music.

"Especially," Maxi had crooned, "if there's not really a plot. She just talks to the band a bit and interacts with the crowd. You just cast a hungry actor – a *good* actor – someone middle aged, and they're just excited to be the lead. They don't care how you fenagled the rights to everything! Just like I don't give a fuck how my car runs. As long as the goddamned thing gets me out to Long Island on the weekends." He had a nasally yet scratchy voice and a leathery, wrinkled hide. Maximos Kladitius was his name.

On one hand, he is the man who gifted me my first real inking quill, and for that I am eternally grateful. On the other hand, he was a master gas-lighter, a word-manipulator, and he wanted me all to himself. Anything I discussed that showed my commitment or passion to the outside world, whether it be a new film or a date with my wife, Maxi reacted like a scorned, insecure lover unraveling at the seams.

It only took a few weeks before I had to push back against

his subtle verbal abuse and emotional manipulation. He picked on me for being 'too nice,' and told me I was too soft with people. He'd listen to me on the phone and criticize every sentence I had uttered. While we were sitting one room apart, he'd poke around on my website – my *personal* website – and then get upset when I wasn't willing to change it from 'Writer & Actor' to production management, which is what I was doing with him. He'd poke at the fact that I couldn't sing or dance, even though I wasn't interested in musicals. He didn't know. He never bothered to watch any of my shit, just tried to pry me away from my creative pursuits and personal relationships. Between that and his tirades about the "snippy little fags"[13] (actors) he had to work with, I nearly lost my head.

"I think that's harsh," I said. "Not a fan of that word, either."

"Oh, please. It's true," was his piss-poor justification.

Imagine my shock when his closest business companion divulged over drinks that Maxi was a recovering coke fiend whose sexual preferences involved pressuring young men of any sexual orientation into for-pay pleasure. He was one of the most homophobic humans I have ever encountered, and yet he was gay… in a sad, suppressed sort of scandalous way. It made sense and was unfathomable all at once. Such things were still considered pastiche.

Society still has so very long to go…

My time with Maxi lasted only two months. He cussed at me and insulted me, and I scolded him like a child. I realized that, the more comfortable he got having me around, the nastier he was getting. I wanted nothing to do with it. There was a whole city of art beyond his dark little cigarette-drenched cave above the famous Sardis.

---

13 Please forgive my use of this most atrocious term – this is a direct quote lifted from my notes to illustrate what a cloven-hooved beast Maxi truly was. Hold not the writer accountable for what's *observed* of humankind – instead, strive to change the world we live in.

That's what Maxi liked to do: he liked to smoke out the world. The world was his tray to ash in and spit in and shit and piss all over. In my younger and more vulnerable years, I had a greater tendency to try to teach people like Maxi a lesson – to win them over. It was the result of emotional PTSD taken in after years of youthful heartache and cycles of similar abuse in my own extended family. I will spend a lifetime trying to forgive human nature. Alas, thus far, I cannot.

"Dogs eating dogs," Maxi had advised me in my first week. "That's all it is out there," he waggled a wrinkly, over-tan hand through his rancid cloud of tobacco, indicating his tall office windows. The glowing marquis of half a dozen theaters on our block seemed to crowd in and eavesdrop on us. "That's what New York *is*," Maxi crooned. "Remember that, and make sure you eat. 'cause no one else is gonna stop and feed you."

I wanted to punch his bulbous, pock-marked, smoke-stained nose. Instead, I turned to my notebook and scribbled, a personal defense since my early childhood… escapism.

My stint was brief, and I still miss that office's legendary view of the St. James Theater on West Forty-Fifth Street. It was strange to walk out on so much professional promise so soon, but my creative spirit was clawing free, and the abuse was stacking up at work. I was not willing to compromise my morals to deal with a shithead like that. So, I walked out on miserable Maxi while he was trying to woo new 'associate producers' he could siphon show funds from.

I'll never forget the way he groveled when he called to beg me back that day. While I was resolved to never go back, I told him I'd think about it and get back to him in the morning. In reality, I just wanted to keep him on pins and needles a little longer before drop-kicking him into my past. His office was a mess, and the longer he waited for me, the more of a mess it would become while he tried to hire my replacement.

Dogs eating dogs, Maxi. Dogs eating dogs.

ଓ ଔ

Back in late June 2013, my phone was still ringing. Saidey's name bounced up and down on the screen.

The motion matched my heart's flutter. However, I thought, I haven't seen her since we said goodbye to each other a year prior, despite a few attempts on my part to email or text her with minor updates… I had kept them minor because I didn't want her to think I was bragging. She acknowledged a few of those, updated me once via text. Had that been in late November?

Familiar tenterhooks sank deep into my heart as I regarded the phone, and I doubted how long I should let it ring. She'd given me nothing to hold onto after that hug goodbye. I still felt her pressed against me as close as she could hold me. Her pink braids smelled like strawberry soap with a hint of Mary Jane. That last scent was clinging to her the way I clung to our Black Swamp memories.

I doubted how long I should let the phone ring. Fuck 'waiting.' I picked up the phone and dropped all pretense.

"Well, hello," I said warmly.

The air was sucked out of the room faster than a breached spaceship. Something was wrong. Her breath was ragged, and as soon as she spoke, the quavering in her voice told me she'd been crying.

11. WHEN I WAS YOUNG

When I was young, the world seemed much brighter. In that world, bad things happened behind closed doors or far, far away. In that world, men understood how to be genteel – that a sensitive side for one's emotions was necessary. These were all things I was taught by my mother. Naïvely, I thought then that all boys had the same nurturing lessons. When I was young, I hadn't yet realized the true cowardice men show around emotions, or the frailty of their precious egos. I do wish these lessons could have come to me another way…

My blood freezes cold still, and adrenaline throttles my system to have to revisit next this most painful, most crucial part of my tale. Humans are animals… and animals are compulsive – to the point of destruction. They take what they want, often by force.

To anyone with a history confronting the darkest deeds of Man, I caution that the next chapter may stir duress within you or rattle loose your own past traumas. Forgive me for taking you there, but Father Time has spared no lashings – he demands I bear witness.

Man tells us it's a dog-eat-dog world.

Man tells us to use brute force.

Man tells us to take what we want.

In many ways, Man tells us to fight back against the very nature of our existence…

Man.
That forceful and accurs'ed state.
The dangle cod with ego's taint.
Who tells us to withhold our tears,
For "Only pussies cry, de Vere."
Man.
Those shriveled rotten little chodes,
Who pant and creep and think they own.
Beware the wolf within your flock,
de Vere seeks to remove your cock.
Man.
de Vere's been in your locker rooms,
huffing those testost'rone fumes.
he's taking notes, he's keeping score,
he craves to pound you through the floor.
Man.
You play too rough for picking flowers,
And so, with you true love just sours.
That's why she grows to hate you so,
Because you can't sooth your ego.
Man.
Someday, your kind will be extinct,
And humankind shall be distinct.
Until that time, shall I lament
The way sweet Saidey's summer went.
I pray she isn't haunted still,
By losing choice – her own free will.
Man.
You stay away, you vile beast.
No one here will let you feast.

Get thee gone, don't read the rest,
For I mean none of this in jest.
My heart still rages in my chest,
And makes me want to kill the rest
Of all the little semen sacks
Who run around and play and smack.
Man.
We cherish so our little boys,
And they never outgrow their toys.
They grope, they play, they get away
With doing whatever they may.
MAN.
It's time to rectify our past:
Our species must strive to outlast
That dangling, stiffy mizenmast
Or else we are all spreading doom
With trauma in each precious womb…

☙ ❧

"Saidey? Are you okay?"

"I'm sorry to bother you like this," she said.

"No, it's no bother," I insisted.

"I didn't know who else to call. I'm so upset… I can't – I don't remember where my wallet is."

"Oh," I stammered, unsure what to make of that.

She seemed far too rattled for a lost wallet.

"Okay," I said, desperate to help somehow, "well, that's easy. First thing to do is get online and check your accounts. Do you have Huntingdon?" They were the biggest bank presence in town at the time.

"Yeah," she sniffled. The sound was small but sad, and I wanted to draw her near, to shield her, but from what, I didn't know.

"They have a 1-800 number you can call to freeze your

accounts." I paused. Air moved around on the other end of the line, so I knew she was there listening. "You should do that immediately, though, in case someone is out having a field day with your credit card or something."

"I will as soon as I get home," she said. "Oh, God, I just realized I don't have my keys." The rustling wind in her phone mic told me she had come about, walking into the wind. She was outside, and she had turned around.

I could hear cars driving by on her end. "Where are you now," I asked.

She hesitated. "I'm on Brüster." Recall that that was the commercialized strip of the grid along the edge of campus. "You know those older townhouses over on Campbell Street?"

"Yeah," I confirmed, "I had a few buddies who lived over that way."

"And you remember the runoff ditch that runs along the road there?"

"Yeah."

"That's where I woke up."

"Hey, hold on," I said. "How did you end up there?"

"I don't… remember…" A brief pause that made me sick to my stomach, then, "I'm sorry. I'm confused."

"Hey, you don't have to apologize." I tried to make my voice as soothing as possible for her: to cradle her in chords, so to speak.

"Jerr, I think I did something really stupid."

"What," I asked.

"Please don't judge me."

"I can't," I stammered. "I would never."

"Okay… there's not a lot I remember…"

My voice steady, I encouraged her gently to share what she *did* remember.

She took a deep breath. "I was at a party last night – a bonfire with the art students. And there's this guy. At first, I kinda liked him – way earlier in the year."

The lump gathered in my throat – that angry monkey picked up its mallets and hammered at the drums of my heart. But I stayed the course. My friend needed me. Saidey needed me to be strong so she could be vulnerable. I cleared the space. Wherever this was going, it was about helping her, not about how she felt for me. In fact, it seemed like she had been spurned somehow and her default reflex was to reach out to me. A very promising morsel my brain tucked away for a more appropriate time.

"But," she continued, "the more I was around him, the less I liked him. I don't need to get into it, but basically, he's a huge egotist and a sexist pig. Thinks he's hot shit, too." She contained an emotional splutter, collecting herself before continuing. "He wasn't supposed to be there… my friend said so. He showed up after a while and he's immediately lingering around me. I tried to keep my space because he knows I'm not interested. He even suggested a date *months* ago and I turned him down and told him then that I wasn't into him that way at all."

"Any specific behavior you saw that changed your mind about him," I chimed in.

"His temper. He'd get aggressively competitive, even with drinking games and shit. Hell, even when he's stoned, he keeps people walking on eggshells. I… I even talked to one of the instructors about it, but he just said 'Oh, he's harmless.' And he wasn't going out of his way to be around me at the time, so I let it go. So, I was caught off guard last night."

"Sure," I agreed. She was her own woman.

"But he's just in my space the whole time. Trying to hit on me, trying to convince me to sleep with him." My spirits snarled like a famished Velociraptor. The monkey imprisoned in my ribcage squawked like a mourning parrot. I was climbing the steepest steel rollercoaster without a security harness, and my insides twisted up inside me as I saw her story reaching its climactic zenith before the big drop.

"So, I left," she said, "but he followed me." A moment of silence. "I think I even told him I didn't want to."

"Saidey, did he hurt you?" My heart-monkey pounded on its prison walls like Travis Barker on a drum kit during a concert solo. I could feel my ribcage cracking with those rhythmic impacts.

The details she shared about that night are not my story to tell. Suffice it to say that the 'man' in question did not take no for an answer, then took it upon himself to try to tell her what she liked. She blamed herself, questioning how much she resisted. Once she'd worked it all out for us both, she apologized.

"It's okay," I said. "It's gonna be okay. I'm gonna help you, okay?" Big words for someone six hundred miles away with no money for a plane ticket. "You are not alone. We're gonna sort it out together."

"Okay, yeah. Thank you… I'm sorry."

"You do not owe me an apology," I said. "But this asshole owes *you* a lot more, the fucking bastard… please listen to me: I'm gonna stay on while you find your keys and make sure you get home safe. But as your friend, I have to be honest with you: no matter how confusing this feels right now, if you told him no, then he forced himself on you."

A knowing sniffle echoed to me over the phone speaker. "I know." Tears streamed freely for just a moment. Then, "I think so. I think I remember saying no a bunch when he was trying to kiss me."

My skin crawled. "I have no doubt you did." Rage boiled my insides to steam; I could feel it whistling out my goddamned ears. There were so many factors preventing me from a drive to Ohio for a quick and murderous adventure, that I know the Universe was keeping me pure. I fear that, to put into words the sick devices I've conjured for that animal boy would surely cause others to have my head examined… or worse. Alas, this is human tragedy: there was no justice for

Saidey. "It sounds to me like you made it very clear over a significant period of time that you did not like him. And I think you should report him to the cops. Not campus police, either – the actual Black Swamp PD." At the time, I was still naïve to the rape culture running rampant in this, our fucked-up society. "But first," I continued, undeterred by the maelstrom of hateful thoughts gathering force on my mind's horizon, "your keys and wallet."

"Yeah," she said. "Yeah, I'm almost back now."

"Cool. I'm right here with you." Could I afford a plane ticket to Detroit? I'd look at finances and ticket prices when we disconnected, I told myself. There were plenty of people I could stay with. Then, there was the challenge of what I'd tell my *wife*, Kelly Joe.

She can fucking deal, I thought. My friend needed help and if I was who she was calling, I had to deliver. She deserved a friend who would drop everything.

"Thank you," she said. Sincerity rang in her voice. "I knew you were the right person to call. I didn't even think about why, I just did it."

'Of course… I love you,' is what I should have said. Instead, I went with, "Of course; I'm always here for you."

She sniffled. It crumbled the firebrick lining the walls of my molten heart. My liquid iron rage at this injustice melted holes in my heart and I felt hatred ignite inside my torso, like smelting iron in those powerful steel furnaces lining all three rivers of my home.

My lungs burned.

My breath was ragged. The molten iron seeped into my brain, and bloodlust of the most primeval concoction boiled my organs. I wanted to scream like some prehistoric terror – a cry so sonorous, its shockwave would be felt by that absolute *Fuck-Rag* in Ohio.

Finally, I quenched the metal inside me. My feelings were inconsequential. This was about supporting Saidey.

With every second spent on the phone, I could hear Saidey's resolve growing back. That bright, bold young woman was showing herself again. Thank God, I thought. Eventually, she would be okay. And I'd be there to support her however she needed.

"Okay," she reported, "I'm back." I imagined the spot; it was on an empty, secluded, flat street, flanked by woods and a modest line of run-down townhouses. I pictured her standing there, surveying the scene with her hands on her hips in the still-crisp morning breeze. The bill of her military cap was no doubt shielding her eyes from the sunlight.

How I missed her eyes…

After a moment, she finally exclaimed, "Found em," and I heard the familiar jingle of a substantial set of keys.

"Excellent."

"That's a huge relief," she said. "But I still don't see my wallet. I'm gonna look closer for a little."

"Why don't I hop off and send you the bank's number?"

"Oh, that'd be great!"

"Just make sure you call them right away. The longer you wait, the harder it'll be."

"I will! Thank you so, so much."

"I'm here all day if you need someone to talk to."

"You're the best."

"Call me back after you deal with the bank if you want."

"I will. Thank you… really."

"Always," I reassured her.

We disconnected and I sent the bank's phone number right away. She never called back that day, and I was desperate not to seem desperate, so I simply texted her around eight that night.

'Hey! Sorry I didn't call. Found my wallet, went home and went to bed. I just woke up.' Her reply came in sometime around one in the morning. I didn't see it until the next day.

'That's all a huge relief. How do you feel today,' I inquired.

'I'm feeling better.'

And that was it. There weren't any text check-ins or email replies. The whole thing shook me to my core. I'd tune it out until I was sitting alone in my thoughts and trying to put pen to paper, and everything would bubble over like unattended potatoes boiling on the stovetop. My soul would shatter as I replayed her call over and over in my tormented memory.

That summer, my writing grew more intense – angrier. I was haunted by my lost muse. The torment of keeping my distance finally took its toll as my brain spun false narratives: I had missed the opportunity for a welcome connection – an adventurous soul who made me feel comfortable. I told myself my cowardice prevented us from forming a proper romance, which in turn put her in the dangerous situation she'd just confronted.

I'd chosen pragmatism – chosen duty – and my choice threw sweet Saidey to the dogs. Denying my feelings for her sealed her fate, I told myself. Had I been brave enough to leap for her a year ago, I might have still been in Black Swamp with her. I certainly would be, I told myself. For I would not have let go readily if she'd latched onto me. I would have stayed, and there would've been no chance for her disaster.

She needed me. My friend needed me, and while I did the best I could, it has never felt like enough. When I think about her… about that phone call… I don't think I'm a good friend… or even a good person. I think I'm a goddamned coward, and I will always be sorry I didn't book a flight to Detroit[14] within the hour. I lived in that silent, horrific reality for ten months more, wishing the world was how it seemed when I was young. Finally, the tides of fate swept her back to me yet again…

---

[14] Toledo had an extremely small, inaccessible, and expensive little airport at that time. The closest international airport hub was Detroit, an hour drive north.

12. WISHING WELL

Now my true curse is revealed – I oft have been the steady foundation others seek for solid ground. But my base grows weary with the pain of these cracks it's amassed under the weight of human consequence in only thirty-five short years.

Perhaps it's something in my own dark and brooding eyes.

Back in 2013, Saidey kept in better touch after that. I tried to give her space – never brought up the things that had happened to her. That was for her to discuss or not: she knew I had her back. Otherwise, I wouldn't have been the one she called.

Over that fall and winter, she texted me pictures of a sculpture she had been working on. It was in several pieces still, and she wasn't sure what to do with it next. She even asked my opinion on a few ideas she had been kicking around once I understood the project.

Those texts got me as high as a bong hit. Saidey was never one to text much, except for coordinating hangout time, so the fact that she texted me *at all* sent my heart-creature into a fit of applause, rattling around in my cage. That heart-creature of mine went about casting wishes left and right. I wished for more conversations with her – yearned to spend time together in person again. Over and over, I'd wish to see her face again.

It only got worse when Saidey informed me she was considering a move to New York. That was in April of 2014. Her plan had been to stay in the northwest Ohio using her local connections to sharpen her skills. She was a year into those pursuits and had the money to relocate. New York City was her primary target. In order to prep, though, she wanted to visit and scope things out. The Whitney Museum had a Biennial Exhibit that closed at the end of May. Due to school and work, she had to plan her trip for the final week of the grand exhibit. She was hoping to stay with me while she was there…

What's more, two days together at a contemporary art museum was the adult artist equivalent of having a teenage crush ask me on a date to the Vans Warped Tour. It was our very own rock show, a roiling sea of potential energy, and my mind told itself stories of smoke, sculptures, and intensely passionate kissing.

My heart sang that day of *the* wish come true. Our flirtatious dance of emotions was back in full swing. What a wonderful throughline the fates had woven for us both! I needed more friends in the desolate and steely stone barrens of Manhattan. And this wasn't just any friend: this was the person whose face I day-dreamed about until I was sure I'd forget what she looked like. I have always been prone to deep and self-loathing rumination, and Kelly Joe was gone so frequently that I completely withdrew into myself for months on end. I worked, came home, and wrote. My writing got me nowhere, and so I read about writing, kept all my notes to myself, and picked up all kinds of odd jobs in showbiz. It was all *technical* theater and film work, meaning it stimulated none of my creative desires, but it paid the bills and had me Broadway adjacent.

Kelly Joe, on the other hand, was spending more than she was making in order to take traveling music gigs as a glorified performing minstrel. She was a one-trick pony who refused to do her tricks for a full year before finally caving into reality. Her nonunion regional theater gigs paid practically nothing, but they offered points towards her union-viable card and status, which was necessary before getting an actual union card. It took some kids a decade to get out of that first phase, but Kelly Joe always had an axe to grind, so she sat at the grindstone and got her union-viable status in under two years. But she did it on our dime, even though her parents were there and willing to help her with such things. We always paid for it out of the money we were supposed to be using for our livelihood.

Finding that she hated living in the city that she insisted we move to, her goal was to be gone on gigs in other, more charming parts of the country as often as possible. Unlike every other couple in theater, she was not interested in helping her husband get hired so that he might join her.

So, I was lonely, and all too anxious for Saidey to join me in Old New Amsterdam. I couldn't have picked a better person to help stay my bouts of boredom – perhaps to even free me from the misery of that minstrelsy marriage. But I didn't want to put that kind of pressure on my friendship with Saidey. I tried to keep everything perfectly innocent… perfectly platonic… but then there was the emoji game.

I realize there have been multiple choices one might judge me for, but perhaps the most blatant flirtation was our emoji game. It was a game we shared that I needs must take credit for inventing. We both had iPhones then and somehow, through our conversations planning her Manhattan scouting mission, the emoji use was concentrated enough that I made a joke about Pictionary. Then I told her to guess what I was trying to convey. I sent her the following combination: A Queen, a cow, and a bathtub with the shower running.

'The queen's milk bath in that awful *Snow White* movie,' she exclaimed in reply.

I replied with the 'thumbs up' emoji and the sunglasses smiley face.

'Ha! Let me try…' Her next text was all emojis. A white mouse, a brain, and a city skyline.

'Pinky and the Brain in New York City?'

She replied with the hugging smiley face.

'I can't wait,' I said. A statement of pure truth.

'Me too,' she replied. 'Also my hair's not pink anymore.'

'Well, that's it. We can't be friends,' I typed playfully.

'Haha,' she replied.

'What color is it now?'

'Blond. I went back to my natural color because I was told it would help me find a job.'

'So responsible. What happened?' I'd miss the pink, but it didn't matter what color her hair was.

'Awkward job interviews happened.'

'Boo! That's their problem, but it *is* Ohio. I don't think I've actually seen your natural color.'

'Nope. Been dying it since high school.'

'Whoa, big change then!' Then, I followed it up with, 'Don't worry; you can still be my Pinky.'

'I better be!'

Our game continued. We eventually cycled through all our old inside jokes, then created some new ones. It was graduation season in the city, and I was company production manager for a college in the Bronx with two excellent theater venues, which got booked up by a bunch of the uptown high schools for graduation ceremonies. I was in autopilot at work, my face buried in my phone as I'd disappear down one of those dark and private hallways to send another emoji riddle to my favorite person. I hadn't felt so close to her since our summer in Black Swamp.

Day in and day out, for a month, we corresponded. I was desperately lonely, and I despised every hour between our reunion. Kelly Joe had been gone on music gigs since late

February. She had just booked more summer work and she'd be gone until late August. When she left, she stuck me with the awkward tension coming from our roommates, her older sister and brother-in-law. They didn't dislike us so much as they expected everyone around them to exist within the orbit of their own emotional needs – to make concessions for them while they conceded no personal comforts to accommodate even their closest relations. But that's another story entirely…

The whole situation was perhaps made worse by the fact that they pretended to be responsible and respectful of others… a dangerous air of self-sanctimony bereft of any morality beyond self-service. We humans are little more than megalomaniacal meat sacks under such conditions.

As I said, I was isolated and lonely. I relished the quiet, empty apartment when they were all traveling. At any given time, I was juggling four-to-seven different freelance gigs in theater and film production across every borough except Staten Island. On weekends, my social time was a three-hour smoke-out at Big Jay's. He and Jeffrey Spalding lived just two buildings away, around the corner from me in Washington Heights. They had a three-bedroom walk-up with my high school friend Bart, so that was my social sanctuary away from the 'family.'

It was my respite on Sunday mornings. Though I was writing science fiction, I was also thinking of her. Of Saidey. She'd startled my dormant emotions awake a year ago with her phone call, and the past year had seen Kelly Joe travelling more than she was home. We always argued more when we were long-distance. She was also constantly batting back overt advances from men of all ages in 'open' relationships, then maintaining friendships with them and going out to drink with them after rehearsals. They'd tell her how mature she was. As an actress, of course. Grooming… gag. But I was the asshole for trying to point it out.

May 2014 finally rolled around. For three fleeting days and

two truncated nights, Saidey was coming to New York, and she was going to crash with me. I barely gave my roommates a heads-up. I resolved to sleep on the couch myself and give Saidey the bed, since there was no way to share that wasn't extremely inappropriate. It also made things less awkward for my roommates and for Saidey if I was the one who slept in the common space during her stay.

Kelly Joe was the one who belonged on the fucking couch, I thought spitefully after an argument around May 15th. She didn't feel that I put enough forethought into her birthday present. She was halfway across the country for her birthday, though, so I ordered flowers and mailed her a card to make sure everything would arrive in her dressing room as a surprise on the exact date. It was an opening night, and she didn't want me there. What more could I do?

Saidey's visit crept closer.

☙ ❧

Wednesday, May 21st, 2014.

Thankfully, the month progressed quickly as my workload inflated at the theaters. On the afternoon of Saidey's arrival, I ducked out of work early so I could clean everything and prep the bedroom for her. The stage managers scheduled that week were, fortunately, self-sufficient.

When Saidey pulled up to the corner of Pinehurst and West 180th, I stepped up to the passenger door of her black Jeep Renegade. She rolled the window down with a smile. She was an hour late.

"Hey," she said, her eyes glinting as they met mine. She had just wrapped up a nine-hour road trip, but her high cheek bones were perfectly blushed – not with makeup, just because that's how her face was. Her hair was wavy, shoulder-length and free of its braids. The orange sunset caught the soft pale blond of her hair. In the waning daylight, it was the color of pale wheat.

"Well, well, well," I said. "New wheels?"

"Yeah," she said, "this was its first big road trip."

"Definitely shinier than your last one," I admitted. Back in Black Swamp, she'd been driving a battered gold sedan.

"Also," I noted, "your hair looks great."

"Thanks! After years of dying it, I'm worried it looks tired."

"I wasn't sure what I was going to think without the pink…" I trailed off. She raised her eyebrows expectantly. "I think I like it more," I said. "You're less of a mystery."

Her dimples pushed her cheeks up, and her friendly pupils seemed even bluer with her true hair color. I hadn't seen her in years, and I just wanted to stand there and stare at her and smile like an idiot while traffic roared by on the off-ramps to the George Washington Bridge.

Instead, I shook myself loose and offered to be useful. "I figured I'd help you find parking, then we can walk back here together."

"Sounds good," she said with a nod. I heard the click as she unlocked her doors, and I hopped in.

We parked her new black SUV a few blocks north, near the southern border of Fort Tryon Park, and I helped her with her bags. It took a while. She got in around eight-thirty, but we didn't find a spot until nine-twenty. That was typical in Washington Heights. My sister-in-law and her husband were back from work by the time we keyed into my apartment with Saidey's luggage.

"Hey guys, welcome home," I smiled. "Max, Bri, this is my good friend and former co-worker Saidey. Saidey, my sister-in-law Brianna and her husband Max." They all exchanged pleasantries, then the roommates excused themselves to their bedroom.

"How're you doing," I asked. "Do you need food, or would you rather just crash?"

"I stopped and ate on the road, so I'm good there," she said. "I'm just gonna wash my face and unwind with you a little before I crash, if that's cool?"

"Whatever you need. That was a long drive you pulled today." I'd done that eight-hour drive – from northwest Ohio all the way to Washington Heights – once three years prior.

"Feels pretty good," she nodded. "I'm out here, yeah?" She pointed to our plush brown couch from Bob's Furniture.

"No," I said. "I'm out here. You're in the bed. I changed the sheets this morning."

"Oh, c'mon, that's unnecessary. I am perfectly happy on the couch."

"How familiar are you with Hunter S. Thompson?"

She snickered. "I read *Fear and Loathing* after I saw the Johnny Depp film. That was years ago."

"Then as your attorney, I advise you to sleep in the bed." She chuckled. "Isn't the attorney's advice always terrible in that, though?"

"Don't overanalyze it," I broke into my best Hunter S. Thompson impression. "Just buy the ticket. Take the goddamned ride, man!"

She laughed deep and full. "I missed your voices." The look in her eyes as she said it struck me like lightning.

My blood ran cold.

My heart sprouted its nasty little bat wings and thumped against its ribbed cage. If it weren't for my cursèd in-laws just one room away, I would have taken that as my cue to *finally* kiss the girl who kept haunting the theater of my mind.

"It's good to see you," she said quietly.

"I missed you," I confessed. Lost in the moment, I leaned close.

She diverted her face to my shoulder as she wrapped me in a hug. That had felt like an overt avoidance. To make matters worse, she released from our hug before I did. Admittedly, I could have stayed in that hug for hours. Instead, I let go as soon as I felt her arms go slack.

"I'm just gonna grab my things from the bedroom before you settle in," I explained. "I'll write while you get yourself situated, so no rush. Let me know if you need anything."

"Okay," she said. "Thanks."

I sat quietly and wrote, enjoying the sounds of her presence in the other room as I did. After only ten minutes or so, she joined me quietly on the couch. I asked about her drive, she divulged that she had intentionally cued up Beastie Boys' *No Sleep 'til Brooklyn* as she was pushing through Jersey traffic on her approach to the G.W.

"I know we're not actually anywhere near Brooklyn, but it was about getting hyped up."

"Absolutely," I agreed. "Especially in that traffic, you need something that keeps you amped."

We went over a game plan for the next day. I had the day off – my schedule was clear to be with her the whole time.

"Oh, cool. I wasn't expecting that."

Ouch. I thought she was coming to see me.

"I wasn't sure if you'd want help navigating the city. Plus I need to get out more while I live here," I affirmed. It wasn't much, but it was some kind of recovery.

"Did I tell you I only stayed with the scene shop for one more semester after you left?"

"Oh yeah, why?"

"Well, for one thing, the masters' students who came in after you were absolutely not cool. Ask Danny when you talk to him. He would grumble to me that he wished he could have you back."

"He's offered me a Ph.D. to come back and help him in the shop a few times," I admitted.

Saidey snickered. "That sounds right. But yeah, it just wasn't the same. I realized I didn't have any friends there anymore. Shy was gone, you were gone, and it just wasn't fun anymore. So, I got that job for the art department. Staff position. That held me over while I saved," she said. "Now, I'm ready to get out of Ohio."

"And you're still looking here?"

"Pretty much. I have one connection way out in Portland – through a friend – but I don't know that I'll go that far." She yawned. "Damn. I should head to bed," she acknowledged. We both stood up and I moved to hug her, but she made for the hallway with an awkward wave. "Night," she said with a smile.

"Sleep well," I said. I couldn't focus on writing. Instead, I put my head down and dreamed that she invited me into the bedroom to steal some time with her. Reality was that the poor girl had been driving alone in the car for nine hours, from Western Ohio all the way to Fort Tryon atop the north end of Manhattan. So, I slept on the couch that night, and her beautiful smile haunted my secret romances like the Cheshire Cat haunts Alice from the trees around her wonderland. He doesn't mean to, you see, but that impressive smile, those ornery cheeks, and piercing eyes are a force to be reckoned with…

ꟹ ꟹ

Thursday, May 22, 2012.

The air was surprisingly fresh that next Manhattan morning in Washington Heights. I lived on the corner of Pinehurst Avenue, just a few short blocks from the express A Train. We awoke around eight and got ready quickly. Then, we climbed the hill up to Fort Washington Avenue. The museum didn't open until eleven, but we were leaving before nine. Given our generous timeframe, we resolved to fend for breakfast on the way.

I peeked at a map again to plan our best route to the Whitney. At the time, it was still located on Madison Avenue over on the Upper East Side[15]. Together, Saidey and I descended into the bowels of Metro Transit Authority. Kelly Joe had left her thirty-day unlimited subway ticket at home in case a friend came to visit me while she was away, so Saidey didn't have to spend any money on subway fares.

"Are you sure?"

"Yes, please. This is exactly why we have it." Kelly Joe might have said otherwise if she were aware of the circumstances. While we waited for a train, I plotted our course. "So," I said, "would you like to get to the east side right away, or would you rather mosey over through Central Park on a scenic route?"

"Oh, let's do the scenic route," she said without hesitation. She wiggled her eyebrows, indicating the Magic Flight Launch Box[16] she'd brought with her.

My heart crooned. Good, I thought. More time alone together before the crowded museum. The park was romantic. I wanted a moment to tell her how I felt. It was long overdue. Maybe we'd finally kiss, I suggested to myself. Yes, I fully intended to kiss her when the opportunity inevitably presented itself again. The thought of the repercussions made me feel sick. Not the repercussions with Kelly Joe, but rather the repercussions if Saidey didn't feel the same anymore. I was confident by then that she had been reaching out for me back in 2012, but I had no idea whether that was still the case two years later. It didn't quite feel the same.

We took the A Train down to West 125th Street, then I switched us to the Local C. As we waited on the platform, I realized what she was wearing: it was her 'Save Ferris' shirt with Cameron's image on it. "Hey," I said, "you still have your shirt."

---

[15] They moved way over to 10th Avenue, very near Pier 53 sometime in 2015. It is no wonder to me, for every special place we had insists on moving or being torn down.

[16] This device will be explained in more detail later in the chapter.

"Oh, yeah, there's no way I'm getting rid of this," she said, adjusting the straps on her retro Reptar backpack.

Our south-bound C Train pulled in, and we boarded.

We sat together. The seats were small, and our legs were touching ever so slightly because we both had shorts on. Just as I thought perhaps she was content with our contact, she pulled away. I told myself not to read into it – there was no need to overanalyze. If I did, I'd develop an awkward social cramp and miss the fun of the moment, I told myself.

Just focus on the moment. Focus on her, I told myself.

Her Ferris shirt catapulted my heart back to 2012. Fuck it. I remembered how I felt the previous year listening to her cry over the phone. I had decided then that if I ever saw her again, I wasn't going to let myself hesitate. I was going to tell her how I felt. I'd be a perfect gentleman about it… a perfect *married* gentleman, but then, she was edgy and unconventional. I had a hunch she didn't care. After all, I *was* engaged when I had received her blatant late-night text: *I'm bored. U up?*

I smiled at her as her eyes shimmered under the flickering overheads of the C train. Nothing could mute their striking presence. If eyes were truly the windows to a soul, hers was as clear and pure as the finest glass.

At West 81st Street I stood, preparing to disembark. My intention was to forge a path through Central Park – full of trees, narrow paths, and corners to cut – ideal for utilizing the Magic Flight Launch Box… and perhaps for stealing that long overdue kiss. Two days and two nights, I reminded myself. That's all the time I had left with her. "This subway stop spits us out right by one of the entryways to Central Park," I told her.

The train's breaks squealed. We stepped up to the doors and grabbed the overhead handgrips as the train shuddered to a halt. Up the stairs and into the crisp spring air we bounded. The morning sun cast a golden haze on the world above as we climbed out of the muggy subway tunnels. We crossed Central

Park West and ducked into the park. I pointed out the John Lennon mosaic on the ground as we circumnavigated it, then revealed the Dakota Building behind us, where he'd been shot.

Lennon's ghost must indeed be with us, I thought, as Saidey responded, "I'll get the Launch Box out once we're further inside."

"No rush," I said casually. "We're wandering over to the East Side, so there'll be plenty of opportunities."

At that point, you could still be fined for public possession of marijuana in New York City. Even though it had been decriminalized back in the 1970's in quantities of twenty-five grams or less, police could still write a ticket, confiscate everything and, most importantly, give you a really hard time about it in the process if they didn't like you… and I *knew* they didn't like me. So, my implication of 'opportunities' meant privacy. My heart pounded like a dying bird as I considered my premeditated infidelity and law-breaking.

"It's so nice out today," Saidey observed, interrupting my anxious musings. Indeed, the temperature was perfect. It had done nothing but rain earlier that week, and Central Park still ushered around pools and puddles in all her nooks and crannies, keeping the air cool in the strong morning sun.

As we made our way east across the park, Haley produced her Launch Box and packed it. She slung her blue Reptar backpack over her shoulder, the black Save Ferris tee providing a perfect backdrop for the pack's multicolor pattern.

"Thanks again for letting me crash," she said excitedly. "This exhibit is going to be really rad. One of my teachers was telling me about it. Apparently, the museum went all-out for this Biennial event. I was looking at their website – there's a real focus on 'interactives'. Also," she added, holding up the Launch Box, "ready when you are."

We found a dirt trail into the trees, then pulled over once we were alone. Saidey loaded the battery of her Magic Flight and took a hit. Then she handed it to me.

"Oh, I'm gonna need some coaching with this thing," I said playfully.

"Yeah, here, let me show you," she said, holding out her hands. I passed the piece back to her. It was a little rectangular wooden box with hieroglyphs carved into it. It measured only two inches long by one inch tall and one inch wide. There was a clear plastic lid that swung round on a hinge, and a little wire basket inside for vaporizing finely-ground flower. A Nickel Metal Hydride battery was inserted on the side, and the user took a slow draw, inhaling gently for a 'hit.' Saidey demonstrated for me, pointing out how the vapor gathered like a little cloud in front of a little orange 'power' light in the device's chamber.

"Just don't suck too hard, Brain," she jabbed playfully.

"Please," I jabbed back, "I've been sucking since 1987." Self-deprecation was an unfortunate special feature of my humor in those days.

Saidey shook her head with a smile and rolled her eyes. Okay, don't shit on yourself, I noted, discouraged by her reaction. I didn't want pity chuckles. I wanted the sheer bliss of the moment… *any* moment… that we could share.

She handed me the Launch Box and I followed her example. Within moments, a friendly, sweet taste tickled my olfactory, and suddenly it was a little easier to be me in the world. Emboldened by that vaporous elixir delivered by my Baroque Post-Modern Punk Rock Venus, I smiled. Her eyes were less intimidating as they met mine with gentle but fierce depth. "Oh, that's pleasant," I said, still tasting the vapor as the flavor of the week.

"I think it tastes a little like peanut butter," Saidey said.

"Yes," I exclaimed without raising my voice. "You're absolutely right. It's like the aftertaste of a peanut butter and jelly sandwich."

"Oh my God, yes! That's what it is!" She laughed, her dimples calling to me as the sweet little wrinkles at the edges of her eyes puckered, agitated to life by my comedy. For a moment, it was just like before. And, though there wasn't a clear path for me anymore, I suspected a kiss wasn't *impossible* once our chemistry had more reaction time…

She tucked the Launch Box away as we heard a pair of teenagers shuffling through the foliage, drawing near. As they appeared, they regarded us in our little wooded nest and snickered as they passed quickly by to restore our privacy. Saidey blushed, the fair skin of her soft cheeks blooming their familiar petunia pink. Still Pinky, even without the hair. My heart sighed, settling in my chest like a freshly fed critter.

In the park, I couldn't find a moment. We chatted and shared and caught up and waxed poetic with her weed. We laughed and eyes lingered while diaphragms chuckled, but there was no unnecessary physical contact, no hopeful look in her eyes anymore. Meandering as I wallowed in this conviction, we ended up outside the museum on the Upper East Side before long. In line, someone mistook us for a couple.

"Excuse me, sir? Your girlfriend's bag is open." She'd forgotten to zip up after our pitstop in Central Park.

"Oh, I – uh – thank you," I said reflexively. Realizing he meant the two of us, Saidey hid her gaze under the bill of her military cap and zipped up Reptar.

"You are welcome," he was a black guy with a Caribbean accent, and he was extremely polite. He held up a camera and badge. "I'm with the museum; may I take your picture?"

We both mugged the camera a little but cooperated.

"Thank you," he praised, "such a striking couple. You are lovely together."

"Oh," we uttered as one, but he was off down the line before we could correct him. I didn't want to correct him. I wanted to use it as an excuse to say just that: 'I think we'd make an awesome couple, and I want to it try if you're interested.'

Never mind your marriage, you child, some voice of reason hissed. Was that my conscience or one of my Black Swamp ghosts?

"Do we actually look like a couple," Saidey questioned quietly to herself as the que ushered us into the open chambers of the Whitney's visitor center. My heart sank as I considered her strange tone.

I redirected my focus to buying her tickets. We used my zip code to get the NYC citizen ticket prices. I got us three-day passes at the local price and wouldn't let her pay. It gave her access to everything.

Once paid for, we situated ourselves in the lobby and made for the stairs so we wouldn't have to wait for the elevator. It was only four floors, and the first floor was just the lobby, gift shop and a modest food court. Yes, the old Whitney location was relatively small compared to the milestone museums I had already explored multiple times. It was much more intimate, which I preferred.

Those two days happened in a whirlwind, and I wish I remembered more of the specifics. I was enthralled, not just by the art, but by the artist sharing it all with me. Hyper aware of my proximity to her, I tried desperately to play it cool.

She wandered off on the second floor, so I forged my own path. I was first mesmerized by the installment titled *Midway Shopping Plaza.* It was a skyward-pointing arrow filled with a grid of business signs from an Asian American neighborhood. From there, I turned to the info plaque for the neighboring piece: *Regarding Venus.*

How apt, I thought. Mention of the feminine celestial body made me think of the young woman I was there with. Though, I pondered, if she were a celestial body, she'd be Neptune, for she often had her fun in the dark, out of Sol's light. Her eyes burned the icy blue of Neptune, too, and there was no question I followed her, sharing a strange orbital dance. I was her Pluto, and in the last two years, we'd switched orbits. Pluto was heating up and Neptune was cooling down, forever tangled in their gravitational dance with the sun, never able to converge, to swing round and round each other for a change. Always in concert, always dancing, but never quite together. Yes; like the planets Neptune and Pluto, we were held away from each other by stronger forces…

ଔ ଓ

We took a lunch break, departing the Whitney around two. We got gyros from a street cart and ate them in Central Park, found another spot in the trees where we could use the Magic Flight, then returned to the museum. I strained immensely to find a moment together, but any time I grasped one, Saidey seemed to raise a red flag.

On the way out of the park, she monologued about how attractive the burly blond lead in that *Vikings* drama on History Channel was. There was an ad atop a cab that prompted this. Apparently, that was her 'type.' Fuck me, I thought. Not at all my shape or build, particularly then, at twenty-six.

Then, there was the supervisor or mentor or whatever he was who she discussed with me. She divulged to me her crush, suggesting that it wasn't an appropriate situation despite their close age. It wasn't until the week after she left that I realized she may have been describing our own situation, but I wasn't listening. I wanted to – but it hurt too much. I was missing out on something special with her, I knew it – our continued fun and friendship kept proving that to me.

In my mind, these conversations were Saidey's way of subtly 'letting me down gently.' Her tone as she shared made me feel like some girlfriend at her slumber party. Excellent! Was I going to get the 'we're just friends' talk, too?

The day went on, as did our time together. Our conversations at lunch left me feeling self-conscious about how much I had been at Saidey's heels since her arrival. I hadn't really asked if she wanted me to join her both days, I just cleared my schedule so I could be with her. That felt creepy as I considered her autonomy.

Was I coming on too strong?

When had I lost her affection?

Did any of it fucking matter?

My thoughts carried on like this even after we had moseyed back up to The Heights. That night, we visited Big Jay and introduced him to the Magic Flight, then watched *Mystery Science Theater 3,000* at Saidey's request. I curated the selection with Big Jay's help, and we landed on *The Pumaman* from 1980. I cackled like a whooping hyena at the ridiculous theme song, which made Saidey laugh at me in disbelief. Big Jay had to pause the show several times until I settled. I hunkered down after the first thirty minutes, stoned and subdued by Saidey's bubbling giggles on the couch behind me. The wreath of peanut butter and jelly-scented smoke cradled us in youth as Professor Tony Farms was indoctrinated in the ways of the puma.

I remember we did a double feature, but I don't recall what the second episode was. We said goodnight to Big Jay and stumbled back around that picturesque corner at West 180th and Pinehurst. As we rounded the corner onto my street, I shuddered to a halt in the hulking nighttime shadows of the George Washington Bridge.

"What're you doing," she inquired gently.

"I just realized what a nice night it is." Bullshit, of course. I just wanted us to stop walking. We held each other's gaze and I prepared to divebomb for her lips.

She broke eye contact. "C'mon, I'm tired," she appealed, moving along. We rounded the corner back to my place.

Yet again, nothing happened.

Yet again, we slept in separate rooms, just one wall away.

What had changed?

Finding that window for a kiss had never felt so difficult. Shit. I felt my rejection probability rising, and it churned the chemicals in my gut.

Pathetic, Gerald.

☙ ❧

Friday, May 23rd, 2014.

The next day, I took even more distance, hoping it might draw her to me, thus informing me further of her interest levels. I had to change my strategy: I'd been on the poor girl's heels all day yesterday. So, on day two, I dove headfirst into the exhibits. In particular, there was a six-hour experimental documentary film about shell-fishermen from up north, in Maine. I sat in that room for so long, she actually had to come find me twice. She moved on again as soon as she confirmed that I was entertained.

There were some exhibits that incorporated postcards and notebooks from vintage sources, and others with old appliances and school supplies. As a vintage toy & antiques hunter, it appealed to me to see such articles considered for museum curation, along with how and why the artist used the materials. I wish I could recount more of the exhibits, especially the ones Saidey enjoyed enough to point out. She noted the originality of their presentation. Back then, her interests were in museum curation, so many of her notes leaned that way.

Every so often, she would come find me, but I kept a wide birth when left to my own devices. It hurt – all I wanted was to be with my friend, to laugh with her and listen to her thoughts on each installment. But I had been a clingy, desperate, (married) nerd yesterday. I told myself to leave her to her fun.

At some point in the afternoon, I even lied about an issue at work and told Saidey I had to shoot up to the theaters in the Bronx. It was simply to give her space. Thursday's signals had left me feeling discouraged, and I needed to back off. She'd never been to New York before and we hadn't seen each other in two years, and I was so desperate to just be in the same room again. But I wanted her to be able to enjoy the museum independently. I didn't ask what she needed, even after realizing what I'd done. Instead, I left for Central Park around one in the afternoon, intent on killing at least ninety minutes.

Kelly Joe was pestering me via text about something during her rehearsal break, so I addressed that.

'Can I just call,' she texted.

I called her without replying. What was the point?

For nearly an hour, I paced the edges of The Pond while we went back and forth about the logistics of some unnecessary trip home she was trying to justify.

Once that was done with, I texted a friend back home who I was coordinating plans with. Sometime in all this mess, one of my childhood friends, Coleman Josephs, lost his father to cancer. It all happened within a six-week span, and I had missed the funeral the week prior due to work conflicts. So, I was trying to return home to spend some time with him while he processed his loss. As we talked, it struck me. Perhaps I could buy myself more alone time to bond with Saidey if I could ride with her back to Pittsburgh. I told Cole I'd see what I could arrange, and just in time.

Girthy rain clouds unleashed a few warning shots as I ended the call: lazy droplets that splashed wildly as they wetted the Park's eastern sidewalks. That initial volley chased me back to Saidey and the cover of the Whitney. As soon as I made the lobby, the clouds ripped open, thundering off the Whitney's roof. Angry lightning flashed in the tiny windows on the third floor.

Once I returned, I could tell her attention was on the art. She was enthralled in every room and seemed to want to walk around and show me a few things. The storm didn't die down until five, but the Whitney was open until six. We stayed, then took our trip across a very soggy Central Park, making our now-customary pit-stop to use her Magic Flight.

The world around us was perhaps the most enchanting I'd ever seen Manhattan, doused in clinging mist that shimmered in the thick air like stardust. The sun felt skittish, ducking away when it saw more dark clouds rolling through.

When we sat down for dinner back over on the west side, my vision telescoped like a Hitchcockian Hallway. I had unwittingly delivered us to one of Kelly Joe's favorite Mexican Taquerias on the Upper West Side. I hadn't recognized it; I'd been too busy staring at Saidey's reflection in each puddle of late spring rain.

I said nothing about the dining spot, just acted like it was a place I knew and liked. Ironically, I'd find myself back on that same patio one calendar year later trying to salvage my marriage. Funny how the Universe works.

On the way uptown that evening, I asked Saidey if I might join her for part of her return trip. I explained what had happened with Cole's dad, and why I wanted to be there for him. I reassured that I would help with gas and tolls to make it worth her while. The stop in southwestern Pennsylvania added at least an hour to her drive, so I didn't want her to feel pressured.

"Oh, uh… yeah, sure," she said with a hesitant nod. "I'm cool with that." But I wasn't sure how much she meant it. In her presence, I was disappointed to admit that it felt like our flirty little dance was finally over.

13. PLEASE TAKE ME HOME

Saturday, May 24th, 2014.

I couldn't believe it.

Six whole hours in the car together, and she was 'cool with that.' It wasn't, 'I *love* being together,' but after all the false-starts and red flags on her trip, it was something.

"You seem like a good friend to have on a road trip," she added thoughtfully. It was meant as a compliment, but my brain fixated on the label: 'friend.' Just have fun and be yourself, I reassured myself.

More than anything, I remember the music. She was curating a 90s pop, punk, and hip-hop playlist for long road trips. I was able to suggest and receive approval to add at least six tracks. More distinctly, I recall us rocking out to the tracks of Beastie Boys' *Licensed to Ill* and later being pumped when American Hi-Fi came on.

"She paints her nails, and she don't know… he's got her best friend on the phone," the Renegade's speakers wailed.

"Fuck yeah, I haven't heard this in forever," I blurted out.

Saidey cranked it as she zipped us down the Jersey turnpike. We sang along to the whole thing – that happened with a few Blink-182 songs, too.

I couldn't help myself. The window was there – her playlist already had *All the Small Things*, *What's My Age Again*, and *Feeling This*. I tossed in *Rock Show* and *Dammit*, and without knowing it, she showed respect to two of my absolute favorite songs – two songs that Kelly Joe couldn't shit on enough. If it was made in the Eighties, Nineties, or later, and it had men singing, Kelly Joe accused it of being 'boy band music.'

"Are you open to a couple more Blink songs?"

"Hell yeah," she said. "Not back-to-back, though. Mix them in?"

"Aye, aye, Cap'n."

She laughed. I wish I could have read her mind, the way she smiled at me then. Whatever thought transpired, it would have revealed everything about how she felt for me. We talked most of the way – there were a few long moments of silence – even a spot where I fell asleep.

I snorted when I woke up.

Saidey died laughing. "Oh, my God," she carried on, "I can't see. I have tears in my eyes."

"Are you okay?" I sounded way too alarmed. It was a reflex. The driver had just told me she couldn't see well.

"Yeah," she made a 'who' sound as she composed herself. "Damn, that was funny…"

She must have noticed that I didn't know how to react. "I guess you had to be there," she added.

"I was!"

"You were sleeping!"

"I'm sorry – I'm a terrible co-pilot." She was teasing, but I shifted gears and got sincere. Unfortunately, it's what I do.

"I'm only teasing," she corrected.

My heart drop-kicked itself into my ribs.

The afternoon sun danced off her dash and her hair – her pale blond hair with its dark roots – glowed pink in a trick of the light.

I'd kill for a picture of her in that moment. Just to go along with my stories – to preserve one moment of the happiness that flourished in our friendship. As promised, I paid for gas and tolls the whole way to my childhood home.

We arrived at my house – my *parents'* house – around two-thirty in the afternoon. Ever eager, my mom was there to great us, which was probably way too much. But I also wasn't a teenager anymore, and I was trying to have a healthy relationship with my folks. Why not let Saidey see that side of me? I wasn't going to try to be someone else with her. In fact, I admitted that her mixed signals could be a result of my try-hard efforts to seem cool and nonchalant. For whatever ungodly reason, she liked me for me.

If only it felt like that were still true.

We offered her a sandwich – offered to let her take a rest before she hit the road again, but she sat for about thirty minutes, played with the family terrier, and talked to my mom a bit about their art degrees. Once we'd arrived, there was no way to discreetly signal to my mom to buzz off. I was hoping for a moment alone. It wasn't long before Saidey decided to move on.

"I want to keep going because I've got work tomorrow."

That was perfectly fair: she wasn't due back home until after dinner. With that, she was off, but only temporarily…

৩ ৩

We kept in touch… loosely, but we did keep in touch. Via text, Saidey asked a bunch of questions about living in New York. It was actually happening; she was moving to New York City. Surely, it must be a sign from the Universe or God or the Reason-Maker of our galaxy. 'The one who kept getting away,' was about to boomerang back into my lap.

The metaphor made me blush as I rode on the subway, trying not to write about her. The weeks between her summer visits were wrought with angst. Kelly Joe was still away on a gig and she hadn't made enough to handle her rent. Meanwhile, I grew more frustrated, and I couldn't get Saidey out of my head. I kept trying to write about all those missed opportunities

– all those delectable little moments of youthful bliss that I hadn't sealed off with a kiss…

How close we came so many times,
And yet our joy felt like a crime.
I cannot find the strength to leave.
I've broke her record, lost the sleeve,
I grew far too weak in the knees,
Doused her flame with apologies.

What will happen when she's here?
Will she finally love de Vere?
Should I risk it; fly the coup?
Were my observations moot?

With her, I never felt astute,
For Saidey seemed so resolute.
We never quite got off the ground,
Because my judgement wasn't sound.
I missed the boat, her candy hair,
But could I somehow persevere?

Please let her come to N-Y-C,
I'll pass the test, she'll set me free.
What of my wife, that Kelly Joe?
What will she say? Where will I go?

I am a corpse, drown'd in my ink.
Of other girls I cannot think.
I want to be Brain and Pinky
Against the world, I am ready;
Together we must disappear,
To Brooklyn, Queens, or Chelsea Piers.

All through June, my mind spun yarns 'round a string of fantasies wherein my own hair changed colors as my heart shifted allegiance. A dozen variants of the same scenario played out each day in my head: Saidey moved to New York, I moved in with Saidey, and the world went on the way it was meant to. Then, after July Fourth had already littered the rivers of Manhattan with fireworks, Saidey texted me a new emoji riddle: an eyeball, a car, and the Statue of Liberty.

I solved it instantly. 'You're coming to NYC,' I guessed.

'Yes! I'm sorry it's super short notice.' She had a visit with a grad program she was considering, and her dad was willing to pay for the trip to New York. He was driving them in, and everything was being arranged around both of their work schedules. They'd be in for just an overnight on Thursday, July 10th.

Other than my work, for I was then juggling a minimum of five freelance theatrical gigs, I frittered my hours away writing about my feelings. I was alone – avoiding my in-law roommates and trying to articulate emotions I'd been tamping down into a rotting two-year-old powder keg.

Secretly, I fretted once more about how Saidey and I could secure time alone. My heart smacked its head off my ribs, riding the winds of anxiety as my mind raced. Why hadn't I risked everything yet? Why hadn't I just told her how I felt about her? Wandering through all those wild exhibits taunted me through dreams. I was forever out of step with the perfect girl for me.

The more I tried to get past it, confront it and push through it, the more determined I grew to tell Saidey exactly what was up with me. It was long overdue, and I wanted to know where we stood. Saying nothing – trying to read her tea leaves – it wasn't working.

I needed to be me – I needed to be direct and own my feelings and tell my friend the truth. After all, if I was going to daydream about being her partner, I had to be willing to risk embarrassment in front of her…

☙ ❧

Thursday, July 10th, 2014.

I met her on the corner of Ninth Avenue and West 46th Street. Sunset had dwindled already, and we had only the wild artificial lumens of a million advertisements, traffic lights and headlamps to witness each other by.

"Hey," I said, leaning in close but expecting only a hug. She leaned wide, keeping our faces from getting too close. We did an awkward dance move of hesitation before she found my hug, settling in for a moment.

"Oops," she said awkwardly, "wasn't sure what you were doing there." A dagger sank deep into my chest. The extra yelp of internal pain told me my heart beast might have just been slain.

We regarded each other with smiles as we separated, and I led her up five old stone steps and into the dark green pub I'd selected for us – the only place I could ever truly claim as my Midtown haunt[17].

"Oh, cool," she said. She pointed at the iron candelabra sitting in the old brick fireplace to our left as we ducked inside. It was flanked by two antique armchairs and a Victorian couch, it was my favorite spot in that bar, and it was available. I plopped down on the couch and encouraged her to join me.

"Pretty empty in here for a Thursday," she observed.

"This place gets busy later," I said. It was Deacon Brodie's, a little Irish pub in Hell's Kitchen where the off-Broadway theater technicians gathered with chill Broadway union counterparts. The place didn't get busy until shows started letting out, which was around nine-thirty. It was only eight.

"That explains why the good seats are open," she said.

"Here," I offered, "I'll hold this spot while you check the menu. But come back and tell me your order. First round is on me."

---

[17] And even still, the place belonged to my close friend Ridge. His name wasn't actually Ridge, but… eh, that's a story for another time.

Saidey raised her hands in surrender. "You sure?"

"Positive… I'm celebrating!"

"What're you celebrating?"

"You," I said. She blushed a bit. She always blushed when I was sincere, I realized. And, I thought, when I was a gentleman. If I held a door or let her go first, my heart seemed to recall a little blush… an aversion of the eyes. In that moment, it felt like a new discovery, for she never struck me as the type to crave such antiquated things. However, I reasoned, evidence to the contrary had been hitting me over the head for two years. I tucked that observation away for later in the night. It was my impulse to be chivalrous, after all. Why hold back if it clearly had a positive effect? "Life would be way more fun if you land out here," I added sincerely.

"I don't know about that…"

"My life would be way more fun," I encouraged.

She shook her head. "Your life's not boring. Look where you live! Your go-to bar is in Hell's Kitchen."

I shifted awkwardly while she approached the bar with a perfectly natural stride. I admired her presence, trying all the while to find a resting position that made me seem relaxed and at ease, two things I did not feel whatsoever. Thankfully, she came back quickly to relieve me of my post.

"Do you know how dark the Belhaven is," she asked.

"Yeah, that's my go-to," I encouraged. "It's like a red ale. You can see through it, but it's on the darker side. Has an amber color." I pointed to someone's glass at the bar. "That looks like it, right there."

"Nice," she said. "Yeah, I'll do your go-to, then." She smiled and sat on the couch, waiting while I ordered confidently. As I returned with our drinks, a gaggle of prim-and-proper actor types charged up the brick steps and through the front door. They murmured amongst themselves, pointing to the empty armchairs, but I plopped down on the Vicky sofa with Saidey and handed her beer over. The actors huffed and found a different spot while we focused on each other.

"Here's to your big decision," I said with hope in my heart. "I hope you end up out here, but I'm excited for you no matter what. Cheers!"

The prim actors, having procured beers, peered longingly at our spot one more time before settling at their table across the way. "It's a good spot," I said, sipping my beer in the dark old tavern with satisfaction.

"It's a great spot," Saidey nodded, settling into the chair and into her beer.

"But we were here first," I said with another sip through my teeth.

Saidey clinked her glass into mine after I lowered it. "I'll drink to that," she said.

"Also," I added playfully, sipping again, "this is *always* my spot. It's not my fault they didn't get the memo."

She laughed.

"So," I segued, "any other questions about living out here?" I had already given her quite a bit to think about via text conversations. Even though it sounded like Saidey had a few loose connections through Black Swamp's Fine Arts program, I also reminded her that I could get her work building sets for off Broadway venues. Back then, I had those connections – was making those decisions and helping to staff crews. All non-union, all scrappy work, but stuff I knew she could handle. She liked working with tools – with her hands. One of her rough edges I loved so much.

"That's good to know," she said. "I haven't given much thought to work while I'm out here, but only because I know there are opportunities with the museums through these grad programs I'm looking at."

I nodded thoughtfully. "Yeah, that's pretty great," I encouraged.

"I had a former teacher put me in touch with a friend of theirs who works with the MoMa, and there was an opening, but…"

"But what?"

She shrugged. "It's been a while since I heard back. Sent them my resume a few months ago. And I want to decide soon because there's already a program out in Portland interested in me. There are museum connections there, too."

Dammit, that did sound cool. Curating art in Portland during grad school sounded like her speed. I fretted New York wasn't going to cut it. It was New York City, I reasoned with myself. Surely, there were just as many opportunities for her out East.

"But then, do I want to be that far away from home," she added thoughtfully. I realized then that I knew very little about her family. I didn't know if her folks were together or separated, didn't know who she got along with better or who she took after. All I knew was that her dad was some mysterious guy in a hotel room a few blocks north, and she'd never ever mentioned him before this visit.

She'd told a few stories about her mom from when she was in high school; I recalled those from our Black Swamp talks. My heart beast howled, saddened at how little I knew about the person I was so obsessed with. She didn't talk about herself when we were together. Her art, stories about friends, but very little about family.

"I will say," I said, sipping my beer, "I don't get home often at all – can't afford to – and Pittsburgh's not that far. And I've paid for flights out west, so I know how expensive those trips can get."

Her head tilted thoughtfully. "Well, Detroit airport is easy to get to," she reasoned.

"And that's only a ninety-minute flight from here," I added.

Her gaze hesitated – lingered on my face.

There was my window. I leaned in for a kiss. Before it even took flight, Saidey broke our gaze, shifted slightly, and took a sip of her beer. I couldn't help but feel like that was to avoid the kiss. It was the gesture that prompted me to have several more drinks of liquid courage. If I was going to be rejected by her, I was going to go out guns a'blazing.

Pathetic.

We spent time catching up, sharing stories, and then we bar-hopped around that side of town once Deacon's got too busy. I don't remember as much as I promised myself I would. I'm fairly certain I showed her where New World Stages was, because I was still proud to have worked on *Peter and the Starcatcher* as a stage crew sub. At one point, we stumbled into one of those stereotypical souvenir outlet stores in Times Square. The overhead fluorescents in there exposed every corner of the truth, and my true love illuminated like a close encounter descending on me in the middle of a lonely field. She zigged around the shelves, pausing to appreciate the Statue of Liberty lighters and the 'I ♥ NY' tees. She bought a few things, speaking of friends back home as she collected them.

The next morning was garbage day for midtown west, so trash bags were piled high up around West Forty-Ninth as we left another of the many Irish pubs in that part of town. As we approached a tiny building storefront tucked sloppily under city construction scaffolding, Saidey laughed and pointed at a nearby pile of trash. She pulled out her phone and opened the camera, adjusting her feet for the right angle as she snapped a picture for herself. We were examining five gold trophies each significantly larger than its neighbors, lined up sentinel along the high Gotham curb, guarding the bags of trash as they seeped their liquid sludge. I had to stifle a gag as the sour tang of the baking trash bags accosted us. Garbage day in midtown west.

Our drunken laughter from the pub burst into a chorus of guffaws as we made confused faces at each other, confused as to the precise lineup of discarded trophies. Was it my imagination or was she playing for time standing still. For a moment, I truly felt the ghost creep back in between us… our phantom kiss from 2012. There was something poetic about the scene, and we both knew it in that moment. Perhaps…

"This place is nuts," she said of New York.

"We could do this all the time," I reassured. "It's always like this." I'd never tried to sell the city so hard. In fact, I spent much of my time there hating the place. I was grateful, but I was depressed… I was focused on the bad things.

Feeling the way she lingered in the moment, I leaned in to make ready, but I kept playing out our first hug that night over and over in my head. She'd ducked away from my face. If I leaned in to kiss her, I just knew she'd hold out a hand and bring me to a halt by placing it firmly on my chest and saying something like, "Hey: it's not like that." Then the night would be over. Not just the night, but my whole youthful fantasy. Sure, I'd apologize, and the night would carry on, but it would be the death of the dream… the reality of the friend zone… and I could see it all too clearly, so hypnotized yet paralyzed I stayed.

A few blocks north of Columbus Circle, I had to pee. So, we hopped the stone wall into Central Park. Nothing like a little trespassing to spark our flame again, I teased myself as I sidled up to the park restroom entrance. It was locked up and barred shut to keep the homeless population out overnight. We resolved to make for her hotel so I could properly use the restroom. Thankfully, they were staying just a few short blocks south.

Nonchalantly, we exited the park along Central Park South and made our way to Seventh Avenue. The phantom kiss seemed to join hands with us both as we laughed together on the avenue. We continued our tipsy wanderings, and I watched her cheeks and eyes dancing their dance. She was happy. She was having fun. And once again, we were together, and we were alone.

My resolve was set; I would tell her how I felt when she

gave me a chance… when we had the opportunity to kiss. That moment didn't come until we were back at her hotel. They were at the Ameritania on Broadway in midtown. We went through the main lobby, and Saidey checked in with the young guy at the desk.

"Room six-oh-one." She held up her room card. "He's with me," she said with a nod back to me. The young guy made eye contact with me, assumed he knew what Saidey and I were up to, and bashfully averted his eyes, that strange glimmer of 'understanding' when one young man believes he's encountered the sexual habits of another bull. I just broke the eye contact, keeping my hands in my pockets as my wedding band grew heavy and awkward on my finger.

With that over, we made our way drunkenly up the elevator, laughing because Saidey also saw the desk clerk's face. Then, we prepared for discreet silence once we reached the sixth floor. There was houndstooth *everywhere*. I said so in an obnoxious upper-class British accent. She snickered.

We arrived outside her hotel door, shushed ourselves and keyed in. Inside, I was surprised to find that the space had a small foyer, which kept the beds in a separate room. That kept lights and noise from the bathroom and main hallway subdued for the slumberous. There was a whole dark rectangle of space for us, I realized as I waited quietly for Saidey to scout ahead. Once she confirmed that her dad was fast asleep, she stashed her bag of souvenir chachkas. She let me use the restroom first, then took her turn.

"I should probably call it a night," she said when she returned. "I didn't realize it was already three. My dad wants to leave pretty early to beat traffic."

A smart man.

There was no other time. I scooped up my nerves. After two years, it was time to tell Saidey how I felt about her. No time like the present. Plus, I reasoned, the liquid courage of my blood-alcohol level made me bold.

"Hey," I whispered, "hold on a sec." I reached for her hands, felt her take hold of mine in response. My heart-bat shrieked with joy and rammed its head into the lining of my chest.

Somehow, her eyes found enough light in the shadows to sparkle back at me like only they could.

I was holding her hands.

We were facing each other. I was shocked by how nice it felt just to hold her hands. They were clammy with drink and, perhaps with nerves, too. I couldn't just kiss her, I reasoned. I wasn't sure she still had feelings for me. She definitely did back in 2012, but so much had changed since then. So, I spilled my guts to her instead, hoping it might prompt something – anything.

"I'm at a point in my life where I've realized how important it is to tell people how I feel about them." A great lead-in, I commended myself. Keep it going. "You mean so much to me, and I want you to know that no matter where you decide to go, I'm always here for you. I'll be bummed if you don't choose New York, obviously, but I want you to do what's best for *you.* I want you to be happy – and I want you to know that no matter what happens, you've got someone out in the world who cares about you. You're never alone: I'm always here if you need me." She was hypnotized, and she didn't break eye contact with me until I took a breath and finished my thought with, "I don't need anything in exchange – you don't have to say anything back, I just need you to know… I love you."

Relief poured from my chest as the heart-creature inside took a deep breath and sat down for the first time since 2012. Then she broke eye contact, and my heart was on its feet again.

Next, Saidey wrapped me up in a hug. I held her there, clinging to the moment like a life raft in the ocean as alcohol threatened to drown the memory for its painful sting right then and there. As we separated, I thought the light revealed glassy tears welling in her eyes. No tears fell, but I saw the storm clouds gather.

The words were on the tip of my tongue as we stared at each other across the lonely darkness. 'I'm afraid I'll never get another chance to kiss you,' my mind pressed. My lips refused.

She hadn't kissed me, hadn't done anything. I had poured out my guts, told her the truth, and my confession seemed to close the door on our emotional journey together.

That was that.

I got what I asked for; nothing.

I went home alone again.

I rode the train after three AM, Blink's *Dogs Eating Dogs* EP bandaging my bleeding heart.

"Home is such a lonely place without you."

'Home,' the subway carried me, back to a cold and empty bed under a barred view of a lonely tree in a wasteland of concrete and stone. I did not sleep that night. I simply lay awake listening to the songs that made me think of her… the songs that preserved that first summer together in all its potential ecstasy. The summer that never came.

I unraveled completely from there.

14. MAN OVERBOARD

So many things we left unsaid,
Between hair colors blonde, pink, red.
Three long years we kept in touch,
Never saying quite enough.
I never jumped, we never kissed.
Her crystal eyes leave me remised,

Haunted, roaming lonely streets,
Weaving through glass and concrete.
Her bright blue eyes, they vex my sleep,
Her hair, hot pink, will always keep
The mem'ry of her smile warm.
Her absence makes my heart forlorn.

I hate myself; I would not see
How Saidey could have been with me.
Broken, sleeping at the wheel,
Fretting just how others feel,
Never concerned with happiness
Convinced I deserved no real bliss.

Jump the current, flip the boat,
For love of God, give up the goat!
This fierce monsoon just won't subside,
Until you've seen behind her eyes.
The siren muse with hair once pink,
The one who forces you to think.
She is the one who got away,
Only in dreams do we still play.
I'm caught in limbo, stuck in pain,
And Kelly Joe thinks I'm insane…

A week later, I bounced from social outing to social outing with different friends, maintaining a steady buzz on alcohol and taking several opportunities to twist that elixir with The Plant. Somewhere in all that mess, my Gatsby-like friend from Israel, Yosef, threw a birthday party. There, a promiscuous siren danced circles round me all night, coaxing me to drink her wine and touch her legs. I was angry with the world – angry with life and angry with my wife, and so the siren barely had to sing. She asked me to ride the subway home with her, coerced me into her midtown lair and had her fun with me. Alcohol stifled my guilt until sunrise, had coffee from the siren's pot, and excused myself as soon as was appropriate.

Regret threatened to dissolve my insides. What had I done? Why had I done that with a stranger but never with the girl I wanted? And how selfish I felt – how unfair to Kelly Joe. Could I tell her? I wanted to be truthful. But we were struggling to get by, struggling to keep things alive between us. I feared the burden of my deeds would be my partner's undoing. Instead, I tamped it down into the powder keg where all my guilt was stored…

☙ ❧

August 15th, 2014.

A few weeks after my fate-less night, during the hottest, nastiest time of the New York year, Saidey texted me an update regarding her future: things had fallen into place with Portland after she returned home from her last visit. She felt bad because she really thought New York was going to be her spot. In the end, though, there were too many possibilities out west for her to pass on.

That was punishment for my sorry escapades in July, I reassured myself. Time marched on, and guilt lived in the pit of my stomach, burrowed into my flesh like some emotional tapeworm.

I gave it up; I fell quite short.
Animal lust – 'twas just for sport.
Regret fulfilled that solemn space,
Where in my heart, I saw her face:
The girl from Black Swamp with the hair
Possessing still her icy stare,
Time zones apart, she fled out west,
To give Portland her very best.
Two years I'd played close to the vest,
Had I scared her when I confessed?

Back to that night, my mind would glide,
Where infidelity ran wild,
And I gave in and was the beast,
Drunkenly chose a carnal feast.
Regret and fear, they festered near
Consuming guilt grew quite severe.
Punished, I suffered; it seemed clear
Fate shook at me Athena's spears…

ଓ ଓ

November 19th, 2014.

Freelancing in tech theater and film can lead to some strange call times, and strange paychecks. One month could be excellent, the next, you work two out of thirty days. The excess of last month becomes the cushion for next. As such, I was prone to make some stupid scheduling decisions from time to time. Hard-up for money right before the holidays, I had taken a few late-night stagehand gigs hanging instruments for a lighting company called IMCD. They handled lights and sound for all the seasonal fashion weeks (there are more than one). They paid great, but they worked late.

That was the first call. Then, that Monday, I had also accepted a morning shoot at the TV studio I was running cameras for. My buddy Mark was the tech director in charge of that shoot, and he promised the call would be six-thirty or later. Back then, I could run on three or four hours of sleep in between gigs, provided there was a long nap when all was said and done. So, I took both, needing the money since I had just wrapped an unpaid off-off-off-off-Broadway acting gig that I was naïve enough to think might get someone to notice me.

The lighting call started at four-thirty and was set to release me at one in the morning. But it was a strike, so they couldn't guarantee that. And since Mark at the TV studio answered to the client we were shooting for, he also couldn't guarantee that late call time[18].

During my commute downtown, Mark texted me. The clients had scheduled live hits starting at six, so call time was going to be five-thirty.

Shit. That wasn't enough time to go home and sleep between gigs. Fuck it, I thought. I'd see if I could stay up. Then, I reassured Mark I'd manage, thanked him for his consideration, and pulled out a notebook. I snuck in a

---

18 Indeed, six-thirty was considered a late call time. We shot live TV product hits for local morning news channels across the country, and our call times were usually between five and six in the morning.

meditative writing session, during which, I wrote:

> *I miss my friend. I wonder if she still thinks of me.*
> *I don't think that's fair.*
> *I should reach out.*

When the lighting crew took a smoke break at seven, I dipped into my phone and asked Saidey how the Pacific Time Zone was treating her. I explained how close my call times were, and suggested that, if she was around after ten at night Pacific, I'd be free for a phone call.

IMCD offered me overtime to stay longer for the strike. I steered into the skid, accepting excitedly. I snuck to the restroom and updated Saidey. It'd be after two Eastern before I got cut from the fashion strike, a few hundred dollars richer but not a bit more fulfilled. As soon as I got to the bottom of the sparse industrial stairwell, through the black metal doors and onto the cobblestones of St. John's Lane, I called Saidey.

That was the beginning of my walk – the longest walk I would ever take in Manhattan[19]. Thank God it was November, or I would have sweated through my shirt. Grinning like an idiot and smiling at her voice, my trek kicked off at Spring Studios. I took Canal Street east into Chinatown, then cut north on Bowery, followed that up to East Houston, then cut west before continuing north along Broadway. Through Union Square Park I traipsed with my earbuds, marched right into the McDonald's on Union Square West, and ordered my late-night Big Mac. It was just after three in the morning.

I was in her trance, thrilled to hear her voice again. Invigorated by her excitement, my exhaustion melted into the backdrop as we shared new project ideas and stories, and our chemistry fizzled even through the vectors of our satellite link.

We kept talking. I took my meal to the second level and

---

[19] Indeed, my entire route spanned approximately 3.6 miles.

sat quietly, listening as Saidey shared. She was in Portland and had an apartment to herself. She was working part-time at a hardware store and part-time at an art museum. She helped them install and strike exhibits.

I congratulated her.

"Thanks! Yeah, I'd like to get in there full-time eventually, but there aren't any openings I'd qualify for just yet. I figure just do a good job and stay dedicated, and then when there is an opening, they'll already know me."

"That's smart," I agreed.

"And I'm already making friends with the head curator there. She asked about my stuff."

"Yeah, and what are you working on artistically?"

"I've been pretty uninspired lately," she divulged glumly. "But," she added with hope, "there was a sale at the hardware store and I get an employee discount, so I bought some materials."

"Like what," I pried.

"A bunch of foam insulation and adhesives."

I snickered.

"I thought it would be fun to use those materials and carve something out of them. Whatever I carve should ideally be informed by the materials. I don't know what statement I could make about insulation… at least, not yet."

"That's a tasty brainstorm I'd participate in," I said.

"Yeah? Maybe we come back to that later," she suggested. From there, I updated her on what I was doing. As I previously alluded, I had done a few roles for shows at the bottom of the off-Broadway barrel. I tried to leave out the crooked shit and the disappointment I had found at every turn because I didn't want to hurl such negative forces into her eager ears. I just wanted to *be* with my friend… to be present with her for that conversation.

In my own pathetic, parasocial way, it was another perfect New York experience… another reason to keep my heart in somersaults. She was back in my life, and she wanted to keep in touch. I thought about telling her what happened in July – how I wished it had been her – but I kept my mouth shut. Hadn't I hurt her enough with the way we drew each other in and then repelled?

Pluto and Neptune in the distant night sky.

From two eastern to five eastern, she stayed on the phone with me. She told me stories from her move, stories about finding work, and she complained about how overcast their weather was. Her updates carried me on a cloud of daydreams, guiding me north to Murray Hill, atop the brent at East Thirty-Fifth and Second Avenue. Once there, I finally docked my rump at the countertop of Gemini Diner, a fine midtown greasy spoon if ever there was one. They were a twenty-four-hour joint, and they were right next door to the TV studio. I ordered coffee and a bagel with strawberry cream cheese.

That conversation left me feeling like there was something open and free about our friendship. It was lighter again, like the flirting friends we were, circling each other back in our Black Swamp days. Eventually, though, it had to end. We wrapped up the call just after five.

She told me to call her if I ever ended up out in Portland. She said she'd been thinking of me lately… even at the diner that morning, I couldn't recall what she said had reminded her of me – had made her think of me a few days earlier.

I held my head up over a fresh mug of coffee, ordered some eggs and bacon, and let my thoughts cloud over with daydreams of Saidey as my vision clouded with the steam from fresh dishes being put away across the bar from me.

It took several days to fully recover from this total denouncement of sleep. 'I'm too old for this shit,' I told myself upon feeling my thick head the next day. Worth it, I reasoned with my id. The city had been alive last night… crackling with our mutual affection as her laugh echoed to me across three time zones.

It was playful.

It was effortless.

It was perfection…

It was the last time we ever talked.

More specifically, it was the last time she answered a message from me. I, in turn, buried myself in Mary Jane's bosom, no doubt a psychological reaction to Saidey's disappearance.

I clung for dear life to memories of her, like they were the last pieces of detritus floating in a shipwreck on the vast Pacific. The big blue was bound to swallow me up, wasn't it? Aye, lost at sea I was, and the waves of my failing marriage were about to come crashing down around me.

And so, I am fully exposed for the true, pure foolish stooge that I am, and not dear Shylock…

☙ ❧

I could keep you here all day,
telling tales of young foreplay.
Or how the minstrel cheated me
By sucking off D. Anthony.
A forty-year-old predator;
Young blondes did raise his temper'ture.
For a full year
Jo wouldn't hear
The warning signs
of grooming minds
that I did say
were there at play.
She just refused
to take the news.
Instead, she went right off her rails,
And lied and told me many tales,
Of all the things she'd like to fuck.
She told me I was out of luck.

We were well-done; She could not see
A way her heart could digest me.

I sowed and reaped what I day-dreamed:
That Kelly Joe would quit our team.
But I could not account for all
The sharp-tongued insults; my downfall.
She broke my will, my self-belief,
Yes, Kelly Joe gave me much grief.
But I've confessed; I earned each bit
Because my heart already hit
Upon another, wilder soul
Whose love still smoldered like hot coal
Within the bosom of my chest,
And so, I never gave my best
To that ex-wife; we were too young.
Kids playing adults grow high strung.

That's long past and I'm much better,
I possess the divorce letters.
My true catharsis is in sharing.
That's how my heart does its repairing.
Now you know, and I can rest,
And in my new life now invest.

Up the critics lunge at me
Challenging the world to see
'Does he not love this girl still?'
Else why wouldst he raise his quill?'
In love anew he claims he is,
Yet here haunts this Saidey Ms.'
de Vere's point is: She's long gone,
This is the last he'll sing her song,
For all strong women, old and young
We must stop speaking all in tongues.
The lesson here, in ev'ry case
Involves some dickhead's forc'd embrace.

I've heard it one-too-many times,
And know first-hand the Devil's rhymes.
'But she was playing hard-to-get,'
Or 'once he starts, it's hard to quit,'
Must we nevermore suggest.
For man's the snake in Eden's breast,
And lo, it seems the pecker's quest,
To defile our very best.
Until I share, I'm haunted still,
It is my ghosts what move my quill.
They have nowhere to lie their heads,
And though their mem'ry turns me red,
It's time they offer forth a glimpse
Of just how close men are to chimps.
They gnash, they pout, they force their way.
Abusively, we let 'him' stay,
He plants her doubts, manipulates.
She blames herself; gas-lit mistakes.
Or else, like jackal, slowly stalks,
No thought beyond his reject cock.
He who would invade a nest:
The Devil beats in that man's chest.

Round and round, my anger surged,
My mind did fall: all good thoughts purged.
Within me, deep anger waged war
And this Brain broke; Man overboard!

I hate this life
I hate this mess
If only then I could have guessed
How much duress
hammers my chest
Just because I didn't act.
I couldn't leap;
Got her attacked.

I hate myself.
I didn't fight,
For her young heart.
I overthought 'doing things right.'
They say regrets you should have none,
But I cannot release this one.
Oh, God, it hurts like knives of heat,
My ice runs cold, my will is beat.
I admit mental defeat.
Help or don't; it matters not.
This is my burden: my heart's lot.

15. GHOST ON THE DANCE FLOOR

It has taken me a decade to confront Saidey's ghost… She moved on, and yet she haunts me still. I never heard from her again after that hopeful November night in 2014.

I tried, though.

I emailed and texted when Kelly Joe was cheating on me, driving me away on purpose in early 2015. Part of me hoped I might bury myself in a new relationship to escape my other pain. How foolish that would have been.

She never responded.

And thank the heavens for that. If I had fallen in with her under those pungent circumstances, it would have no doubt torched the summer gleam around our memories in Black Swamp, charring them beyond recognition the same way I have since lost good memories that included too much of ex-wife Kelly Joe.

After those attempts to reconnect while my world burned in 2015, I decided to politely buzz off and leave Saidey to live her life while I sorted through the bullshit in mine. It hurt that we lost touch, but I can't say that I blame her.

Every 238 years, Neptune grows weary of the eighth orbit

and dances with Pluto, but in the end, Pluto's still the one left out in the cold. Perhaps that's why he sits there in the dark as he's declassified and reclassified. He's waiting for that familiar tug from nuanced Neptune's gravity field, in love with how it promises to make him dance once more…

If I were an astronaut,
Perhaps I'd stop a while,
And console poor Pluto's heart,
Where Neptune has beguiled.

"No more in this lifetime,
"And no more in the next,
"Will you see fair Neptune's eyes,
"Or get another text."

"It's best now to move on,
"There's story left to share,
"Perhaps, though, summarize or skip
"All your ex-wife's affairs."

To divulge the brutal battle scars of my separation from Kelly Joe in full would require another manuscript entirely. Suffice it to say that the whole divorce felt specifically designed by the universe to punish my affection for Saidey.

Beyond that, those woes are inconsequential.

While Saidey and I may have never had a physical relationship, the truth is we were emotionally entangled in a very complicated way… in a way that suggested infidelity. It was an intimacy of thoughts and special moments as bonding as any kiss might have been.

In short, it was inappropriate given the relationship I was already committed to. Far more to the point… we were all too young to know any better, so it doesn't do much good pointing fingers, either. Not often in my life has my father felt the need to offer, let alone repeat advice, but when Kelly Joe and I were about to get engaged, he kept reminding me how young we were and asking if I was certain. His concern was simply that neither of us had been out into the wide world, and his intuition was dead-on: we were just young. A bit *too* young. As a result, we erupted, spewing our ash all over those who dared to trespass on our emotional island…

But there's hindsight again for you.

ᘓ ᘐ

Black Swamp University, April 2022.

I was in town for a whopping three days, my first visit back to that boggy little town since I swam away a decade earlier. During my short stay, Black Swamp had demonstrated all of its weather: rain, sunshine, overcast, snow flurries, a spot of hail, and, of course, plenty of wind. Just as I remembered it.

There was a moment, a quiet one on my last morning in town, when I snuck over to U-Hall by myself. Edwyn was in town with us, and he would entertain our former educators and my lovely (second) wife for a few brief moments, I reassured myself. There was no need to have company for this pathetic little pilgrimage.

The walk across campus was enough time for rain clouds to roll in and obscure the golden sun. Suddenly, a chill hung in the air, the kind that reminded me I was visiting a grave. The sensation bit at my lonely bones all the way to the 'new and restored' University Hall. I saw the hole in the sidewalk where my beloved shop had been. They'd moved Admissions, gutted the shop and the Joe C. to make room for more lawn and gently sloping concrete steps.

The shop and the Joe C. were just a concrete landing five steps up from the lawn. I tried to appreciate the green space.

My head spun. I was surrounded by ghosts – visions of my friends, of years gone by, of shows performed. Of nights hunting for Alice with a pink-haired punk, a girl I hadn't thought of in nearly eight years.

I ducked around a corner, out of view of the windows for the Admissions office, which, I noted, now occupied the old Saint Eva's lobby. I took a hit to ease the pain, and, in my gently altered state, I climbed the steps, halting just outside the new entrance.

I turned around, overlooking the unceremonious grave where my college theater career was buried. Wind and a singular gust of rain ripped through the campus alley at that moment, amplified because the theaters weren't there to shield the interior lawn. That had to be awful in the winter months, I pouted.

For a moment, I felt empty once more. I pondered the hole in space where the theaters still stood in time, revisiting more memories of shows performed and legs well-broken. Those fond recollections did nothing to fulfill me. All they did was rip the hole in space wide open. It was a void on campus: a black hole that had swallowed the living light of my sweet stages. Empty, pointless memories… lost to time under the shovel of a bulldozer and a cement truck's trough.

I imagined the proscenium as it had been, walked what had been the stage's length along the entryway steps, then went in to see the rest. The chill of AC caught me off guard. Something clicked. There, where Admissions spilled into the main hall, a drop ceiling and fluorescent lights made me feel exposed. My memory knew the balcony had been there, and I crossed out into the building's main hallway. They'd plucked out a few of the Greek columns on floor two and opened up the space.

My heart sank.

Empty.

Sterile.

Soulless.

Soulless. That was it! That was the emptiness. The space

where those stages once stood had been U-Hall's heart, and Alice had been its soul. Alice was gone. That's why the void felt so apparent. She never stirred to greet me, never made me feel uneasy with the cold kiss of goosebumps on my neck or arms the way she always did before.

She wasn't back at the Foxe Center – I never once felt her there – I knew she'd kept her word. She hadn't wanted the new stage any more than I had.

Alice, my last connection to Saidey, was also gone. Dead, in an even truer sense of the word. They say ideas are harder to kill than living things. Ghosts are somewhere in between, so I'm not certain where their mortality lies, but I know this: there wasn't a story on anyone's lips about a ghost in the wedge-shaped Foxe Center.

I shook my head and turned back. It was too much to bear, and I thought I might need to cry. Outside, I ducked around the corner to take another hit and regain my mental footing. I disguised my smoke as a tour guide appeared with a group of high schoolers and their guardians. They were headed for the Admissions office in my Saint Eva's gutted carcass.

A teen girl in all black with horn-rimmed glasses, thick eyeliner and a beanie asked, "Isn't there supposed to be a ghost in the campus theaters?"

"Not anymore," said the tour guide. "The current theater building is only ten years old," she explained, "but we're actually standing where the theaters used to be. Apparently, that part of the building did have a ghost. But no one has seen a ghost in the building since they did the renovations."

The teen girl frowned. "Oh, bummer."

The tour guide hesitated, but she was clearly with a group that made her feel comfortable, so she leaned in. "If it's ghost stories you're looking for, though, ask some of my co-workers," she pointed to the Admissions offices. "Everyone who works late has seen a glowing white light floating out here in the courtyard... in mid-air. And everyone says it's not consistent. It flickers like a dying lightbulb, then stays on steady sometimes, then blinks out again just as abruptly."

The smile creeping across my lips was involuntary.

"Personally, I think it's a theater light. Like, a ghost of the stage itself. Shoot, what's the name of that light they leave on?"

"A spotlight," one of the kids offered demurely.

"No, not that," the tour guide said.

"The ghost light," I called out over my shoulder after I had started walking away.

"That's it," exclaimed the guide. "Thank you," she called after me. I waved over my shoulder in acknowledgement, then turned away so I could take another hit and settle my heart. The ivy stank of indica kissed my nostrils as I walked away, leaving my sadness at the side of Eva's grave.

Something cold shot up my spine and I turned back as it finally decided to rain. The familiar smell of teakwood mixed with the peat moss and well water overpowering my olfactory.

Surely, I was mistaken…

No, there it was, the old teakwood smell of the Eva lobby lingering with the stench of drowning earth worms.

Was it her?

Leave the ghost light on for me, I heard myself tell Alice all those years ago. I choked out the tears pressing up behind my nose. Next, I stifled my memories, dousing the lamps on their waltz around my cranium.

As I wandered back to the Foxe Center to say my goodbyes, I wondered if Saidey had been back to hear the tale of the flickering ghost light… one ghastly monument to the time we shared in that majestic old cadaver.

Shielding myself from the wind, I gave my tired heart permission to sooth itself with wandering verse…

So many things we left unsaid,
Between hair colors blonde, pink, red.
Two long years we kept in touch,

Never saying quite enough.
I never jumped, we never kissed.
Her bright blue orbs leave me remised.

From my world, she's long since fled.
For all I know, she may be dead.
I hope she's not, and yet, don't tell,
For writing this put me through Hell.
But let her know of the Ghost Light
That flickers now in Black Swamp's night.

Remind her of the shop and stage
Where we first had the curtains paged
On what life might have looked like when
We first disturbed Alice's den.

There are no more ghosts on that site,
Unless she counts that sad, strange light,
The one that Alice left for me.
Was she a ghost: the girl Saidey?
I'm happy, though it cuts me still,
The pain is frequent: very real.
Did I hurt her? I cannot say,
But if I did, I can't delay,
Apologies are due to her,
From this young and misguided sir.

I loved her then, but couldn't' see,
That she wanted to be with me.
On I blundered, like a mule,
Leading her on like a fool.
Now, her specter lingers near,
Ready to remind de Vere:

Ghosts are not mere specters,
Roaming through the night.

They're lost feelings and emotions
That paralyze with fright.
They bubble in our depths, deep down,
Informing us each time we frown
They build up walls, shut people out,
Until we break down with self-doubt.

Memories as sharp as razors.
Trauma that still shocks like tasers.
The more we hurt, the more we rage,
For in our hearts, true wars are waged.
Pain echoing through time itself,
Pain craving drink from the top shelf.

It's Saidey and it's Alice,
Whose stories grew my callous.
They deserved far better than
To fall prey to the phallus.

Their ghosts live in my heart's frail walls,
Ghosts who do not answer my calls.
Ghosts whose blue eyes still do enthrall,
Forever in my youth's dance halls.

Is it me?
am I alone?
Or are we haunted, everyone?

☙ ❧

Even if Saidey doesn't think of me anymore…

Even if she's blocked it all out and moved on… and even if she's forgotten who helped her through it… I *was* the one she leaned on. I wasn't just some summer fling or ex-boyfriend. I was the person she sought for help.

In hindsight, I think she called me that morning in 2013 because she trusted me and because subconsciously, she knew I *couldn't* be there in person. She didn't want anyone in her space that day, but she needed support – someone she could talk to – someone who was safe – to help her sort it out… and that had been me.

As a grown-ass-man, I can see the signs that she was attracted to me, at least back in Black Swamp. Maybe that changed once I was 'married.' Or maybe, after what happened to her, it was harder to be attracted to me *because* of my connection to her trauma. I cannot say, but I'll take that sentence a million lifetimes over to be the support she deserved on that awful day.

The tradeoff is this poltergeist of partiality that burdens my youthful remembrances. Saidey is the ghost who haunts my story, not Alice. Saidey: the ghost on my dance floor. Saidey: 'the one who got away.' Her struggle chills my bones; her memory ices my veins. Her silence long ago shredded all remaining hope of friendship between us. Just like Alice and her man in tan, we were doomed to end our stories out of pace. Make no mistake, the lust of boys twisted fate's intentions, took a budding Black Swamp romance, and snuffed it out for unlawful carnal knowledge. We were victims to the fallacy of *man*, and so at him, my fangs are forever bared. And so, I recant:

It's Saidey and it's Alice,
Whose stories sparked my malice.
They deserved far better than
To fall prey to the phallus.

Their ghosts live in my heart's frail walls,
Ghosts who do not answer my calls.
Ghosts whose blue eyes still do enthrall,
Forever in my youth's dance halls.

It is not me.
I'm not alone.
We are all haunted; everyone.

ENCORE

...Who would fardels bear,
To grunt and sweat under a weary life,
But that the dread of something after death,
The undiscover'd country from whose bourn
No traveler returns, puzzles the will
And makes us rather bear those ills we have
Than fly to others that we know not of?
Thus conscience does make cowards of us all;
And thus the native hue of resolution
Is sicklied o'er with the pale cast of thought,
And enterprises of great pitch and monument
With this regard their currents turn awry,
And lose the name of action...

-Hamlet, Act III, Scene 1; *Hamlet, Prince of Denmark*
Shake-Speare

ABOUT THE AUTHOR

{photo credit: Dale McCarthy @dmdarkroom}

Award-winning author Gerald de Vere was born and raised in the haunted hills of Pittsburgh, Pennsylvania in a time when technology was a decade behind the trends. In that sense, he has lived a somewhat antiquated life while relishing in the study of history, biology, psychology, and art. He holds bachelor's degrees in English and Theatre, as well as a master's degree in Creative Writing, all achieved at Black Swamp University in Ohio. His debut novel *Creatures* won the 2023 Living Now Book Awards Bronze Medal in General Fiction as well as the third-place winner in Intrigue Fiction at the 2023 PenCraft Book Awards. His poetry has been featured in Altered Reality Magazine. When he's not writing, Gerald enjoys roaming the North American wilderness and skateboarding to annoy the neighbors.

For more info, visit: linktr.ee/deverewrites

The keen observer may have noticed a correlation between the dedication in this book and the chapter list…
The unauthorized soundtrack to this story is available on Spotify[20]:

[20] The publisher makes no claims to the rights of any of this music. The author simply wished to pay homage to the artists who inspired him.

Made in the USA
Middletown, DE
28 October 2023

41373550R00113